Charisse o

Brent took her hand and nodded. "See you in two weeks."

He wanted to turn her hand over and softly place a kiss on her pulse. Would her heartbeat spike the way his did right now at the mere thought of the temptation?

Thankfully, he didn't have to think about the option. Charisse led the way out of the room. She chatted about always being there when the cleaning crew came through. He offered the expected nods and interested tilt of the head as he listened to the harmless topics.

But darn it, her new haircut allowed the tip of a rose tattoo to peep above the collar of her blouse.

"You were saying?" Charisse stopped and turned.

Brent almost bumped into her back. "Oh, I was... complimenting your new hairdo. Suits you." His hand rose to touch her hair.

Her face turned into his hand, perfectly molding into his palm. Before he could pull away his hand, she covered it with hers. Her gaze rested on his face, almost at his chin, before she scanned his face slowly until her eyes met his.

He only hesitated for a second before lowering his mouth to seal the kiss.

Books by Michelle Monkou

Kimani Romance

Sweet Surrender
Here and Now
Straight to the Heart
No One But You
Gamble on Love
Only in Paradise
Trail of Kisses
The Millionaire's Ultimate Catch
If I Had You

MICHELLE MONKOU

became a world traveler at the age of three, when she left her birthplace of London, England, and moved to Guyana, South America. She then moved to the United States as a young teen.

Michelle was nominated for the 2003 Emma Award for Favorite New Author, and continues to write romances with complex characters and intricate plots. For more information, visit her website, www.michellemonkou.com, or contact her at michellemonkou@comcast.net.

IF I HAD YOU

MICHELLE MONKOU

KIMANI™
ROMANCE

For all those with dreams in their minds
and passions in their hearts.

KIMANI PRESS™

ISBN-13: 978-0-373-86251-1

IF I HAD YOU

Copyright © 2012 by Michelle Monkou

Recycling programs
for this product may
not exist in your area.

www.kimanipress.com

Printed in U.S.A.

Dear Reader,

If I Had You is a reminder that we shouldn't discard those dreams that took hold of our imaginations. Dreams take us to a place of possibility and even probability. Any time or any place can serve as the launchpad for those dreams. More importantly, there is no age limit for nurturing those vivid dreams.

Brent Thatcher and Charisse Sanford are two rising stars with big dreams. You can't help but root for them as they work against the obstacles that threaten their accomplishments. Having strong belief and faith certainly provided the fuel for their journey.

So from this day onward, write down your dreams. Think about the action plan. Push aside any fears. Take that first step. And, simply, go for it!

Later this year, another sexy millionaire will stop at nothing to get his soul mate. Each new character is introduced in the previous book—in other words, an enticing cameo appearance. Check me out on Facebook at http://facebook.com/michellemonkou or my blog, michellemonkou.blogspot.com.

Good luck,

Michelle Monkou

Chapter 1

Charisse Sanford, with her head pressed between her hands, stared at the phone on her desk, willing it to ring with new business. At the beginning of the day, her assistant had handed the current list of clients to her. The fact that the list hadn't changed in three months wasn't lost on her.

On the bright side, the names in front of her meant that no one had left New Vision. Given the economy and budget tightening in companies, she half expected her New York public relations consulting service to be bombarded with contract terminations, even at the loss of their deposits.

However, on a bleak note, no new clients had signed on for her services. The scant number of projects in the pipeline made her want to cry. After she'd taken note of the client list and the month's financial statements, she'd transferred funds from her personal money market account to her commercial account, to provide a cushion for the company's expenses.

She had to focus on the pipeline. Going back to work in corporate America wasn't an option. At twenty-seven years old, she'd paid her dues with diminishing returns. Her last company's grudging offer of a promotion when she announced her resignation came a little too late.

Her assistant knocked on the door and popped in her head. "Heading out, boss lady."

"Have a good night." Charisse stretched her arms, trying to ease the stiff muscles leading up to the back of her neck. A wide yawn overcame her. "I have a few more proposals to complete. I'll have them on your desk to proof, and then we can send them out right away." She tried to blink away the exhaustion.

Tracy nodded. She turned away but paused before retreating from the doorway. Her crystal-blue eyes looked troubled.

Charisse waited.

Tracy's mouth tightened.

Charisse's exhaustion rapidly disappeared. Now unease squirmed in her stomach. She already knew what her assistant would ask.

"Any word from Shelby?" Tracy asked, with disdain dripping from every word.

Charisse shook her head. "She said that she needed another month. The company just landed another contract. She'll get a healthy bonus if she stays through the length of the project. Then she'll make the switch and head over to start with us."

"She said that a month ago," Tracy accused. She now stood in the office with her arms locked in place across her chest. "Sorry, I know that she's your friend."

"It's okay." Charisse had made excuses and issued promises to her small staff that all would be well as soon as Shelby joined the company. Plan B had better come fast.

Shelby, her colleague from a different PR company, had become a friend over the years. They'd decided to join forces and start their own firm. Yet, when the time came, Shelby wasn't ready. Charisse didn't let the delay stop her and opened the doors to New Vision, with the expectation that Shelby would follow within the month. One month turned into two, and now six months later, she still flew solo.

"Why is she dragging her feet?" Tracy tossed up her hands in frustration. At twenty-one years old, Tracy was still at the crossroads of youthful brashness and adult work ethic.

"I'll be chatting with Shelby tomorrow. She wanted to get together over dinner."

Tracy ran a hand through her thick curly black hair. She bit her bottom lip, a sure sign that she had more to say.

"I'm as frustrated as you." Charisse aimed to calm down her assistant. Through it all, they had managed to have a friendship that came from working long hours together and commiserating over the brutal nature of the business.

"I'll let you continue to be the optimistic one. Any word about the few proposals floating out there? I haven't had any calls come my way."

Charisse shook her head. "I still think the glass is half full." Her statement hung in the air like brittle glass ready to shatter into a million pieces.

It wasn't on impulse that she had stepped out to fulfill a longtime dream to be her own boss. For Charisse, being happy meant earning money and success without anyone else's help. In college, she was the president of the entrepreneur club. She had pursued many ideas, and when they failed, she grew discouraged. But she always bounced back with a keener edge and stronger appetite to try again.

Her ambitious drive scared off friends—especially boyfriends—and earned her many counseling sessions from her mother. The people around her seemed to want to push her onto their paths—walk their walk. No way. When the opportunity for this company came, she didn't resist. Instead, she'd leaped into the boat that would take her to the prize.

She had a lot to prove now, despite the delay with the full rollout of her plans.

Tracy wrinkled her nose with a small shake of her head.

What else was there to say? Tracy was witnessing the ugly side of small business. The young woman was her first employee when she opened the door to New Vision. They had furnished and decorated the space, then taken photos of each other standing near the silver-plated office sign.

Despite their efforts, clients didn't immediately flood the reception area. She and Tracy, as a result, had spent long days reviewing the business strategy. Each client had to be coaxed to take the risk of signing with a start-up company. In some cases, her former employers had stepped in to provide recommendations to the potential clients with smaller budgets.

Tracy may not have made a financial investment in the company, but she certainly had invested her time and dedication. Her hard work and the constant discipline had turned her into more than a trusted and loyal employee.

"Don't know how to say this, but I have a job interview at the end of the week." Tracy glanced up and then returned her gaze to the floor. "I love it here. You're a great boss, but…" When she raised her gaze, tears shimmered in her eyes.

"You don't have to explain. I understand." Charisse pushed her chair away from the desk and stood. She approached Tracy with outstretched arms and tightly hugged the young woman. "You know that you'll get a fantastic recommendation from me. I'm sure that you'll impress them the same way that you've impressed me."

"I wish that I didn't have to do this. But, Jonas…"

"I know."

"And day care is going to be more expensive because of Jonas's allergies. He can't be around a lot of children until he's much older." Tracy flicked an escaped tear from her cheek.

Charisse nodded. She didn't have a boyfriend, much less a husband and children. She might not have the responsibility of someone being dependent on her, but she did understand living on a tight budget, especially when much of her savings had been used to support her business.

"You have to do what's important for your family. I won't stand in your way." Charisse wrapped her arm around Tracy's shoulders and led her out of her office.

"Thanks, Charisse."

They hugged.

Charisse, with a heavy heart, locked the door after Tracy departed. The cleaning staff usually came around six o'clock, which was in an hour. Many nights she greeted them, even exchanging pleasantries as they moved through the office. The supervisor, when she was on-site, always felt it necessary to counsel about her lack of a boyfriend or date nights.

She resumed her seat in her office and flicked on the small TV on a nearby bookshelf. Her nights were spent heading off to networking events, preparing for the few meetings that she'd managed to wrangle, or following up with busy execs for their decisions on various phases of their projects. Tonight was more of the same.

After Tracy's news, she wasn't in the mood to do anything. The last thing she wanted to hear was the long litany of bad news that permeated the nightly news on TV.

Charisse looked away from the TV screen with a heavy sigh.

The phone on her desk rang.

The shrill noise startled her. She looked at the number displayed in the small screen. Her hand hovered as she mentally ran through possible clients who would call after hours. Finally she answered with fake enthusiasm, "New Visions PR, Charisse Sanford speaking."

"Good evening. Brent Thatcher, here. Calling from Thatcher Entertainment Agency."

"How can I help you?" Charisse searched her memory for any business connection to the agency.

"You submitted a proposal three months ago for the job of PR specialist. My apologies for the long response time, but I'm very impressed with what I've read."

"Thank you." Charisse tried to discern any clues about her chances.

"You've made the short list."

"Okay." She wouldn't get excited, yet.

"I'm interviewing three candidates, including you."

Charisse recalled that this particular project had a lot of potential. The agency had a singing group that could be molded into tomorrow's R & B notables.

"I'm in Boston but will be in New York tomorrow for several days. Are you available for a meeting?"

"One second. Let me check my schedule." Charisse didn't care what she had to reschedule. Thatcher Entertainment Agency had to be her new client. Her business needed Brent Thatcher.

She clicked on her computer and checked her schedule. The blank white space of no appointments glared back at her.

"We can schedule for another time. I understand that I'm contacting you with short notice."

Charisse shook her head. "I don't have any conflicts for the next few days. We can meet." *'Cause I'm desperate.*

"Then, let's make this official. We can set the time, and then I'll have my secretary follow up with an email confirmation."

Charisse agreed.

Dare she hope that she was getting her wish? She had one in three chances to snag this potential client. Moreover, she didn't mind spending a few hours with a man who had a voice like Bristol Cream—smooth, flavored with a Boston accent and rich with nuance.

"How about you pick the day and time, and I'll pick the place," she tossed out. She could fake cockiness in a clutch.

"Tomorrow evening at seven. Please don't worry. I

don't want you to feel that this is a stiff interviewing process. So I hope you have a great place picked out, preferably one that can serve dinner. I'll be coming off the plane and heading straight to you."

"Japanese or Cuban cuisine?" Charisse offered her personal choices. She tried to relax with the swift change to her life.

"Cuban." He paused. "This will be a first. No complaints from me, though. I'm looking forward to broadening my horizons. I'll have you to thank for the experience."

"Now I feel the pressure," she joked. "Although I'm sure you will like the food."

"I'm flying blind on this one. I'll put myself in your hands."

"You won't be disappointed." She hoped.

"With the cuisine? Or with meeting you?" He laughed, low and deep.

"Both." Charisse warmed under the soft, husky laughter. As the words were uttered, she couldn't believe that she was being so bold. Desperate times called for desperate action.

Charisse allowed Brent to end the call. For a few seconds, she stared at the phone. In the snap of a finger, opportunity had arrived knocking at her door.

She picked up the phone again and dialed the Cuban restaurant. Her desire to win drew a smile to her lips. When she finally got the restaurant owner, her dear friend, on the line, she presented her plan.

"Luisa, I need a meal that can make a man want to hire me. Bring out the best. This may be the client that is the answer to prayers."

"Darling, for you, anything. I'll have something special from the appetizer to the dessert." Luisa chuckled. "And if he doesn't hire you before the waiter presents the last dish, I'll come over to your table and beat him silly."

"I appreciate your support, *mi amiga*. Can you also give me a quiet spot?"

"Let's see. That might be difficult. I have the deputy mayor using the VIP room."

"Oh, okay," Charisse didn't want to appear ungrateful. After all, she knew Luisa wouldn't charge her the full price for the extravagant meal. But she wanted to pull out all the stops and show that she had some clout, even if it happened to be with her childhood friend.

Now that she'd taken care of Phase One of her plan, she wished that Tracy was still around to celebrate. Then again, any celebration now would be jumping ahead of any good news. She still had nothing to help with Tracy's needs.

She sighed.

No matter how much she tried to concentrate on the work in front of her, she couldn't corral her thoughts. Resigned to being unproductive for the night, she closed the files and readied herself for the trip home. This meant that she needed to grab Thatcher's file and re-acquaint herself with the particulars of it during her commute.

Brent Thatcher tapped his chin with his cell phone. The conversation had gone well. Charisse Sanford was still available. Although he only had the phone call to judge, he sure did enjoy her direct approach. And he'd get a Cuban dinner out of the meeting—definitely a point for Sanford.

Her résumé had everything he needed for a PR specialist. His notes in the margin underscored what impressed him. He'd already interviewed the two other candidates. None could compare to Sanford. The job was practically hers. However, he had no reason to share this information.

They were both new business owners. He imagined that his tight budget would be offset by her need for business. More so, he wanted someone hungry and passionate. Time wasn't on his side. He had to get things rolling for his newly signed group, All For One.

"Brent, snap out of it. You're supposed to help me hang these curtains."

Brent looked up at Fontana, his sister, who was perched on the step ladder with her hand on her hip. Her frown merely brought a smile to his lips, which earned a harsher glare.

"If you're not going to help, then go home." She climbed down the small ladder and marched across the room toward him. She might be on the petite side, with her head barely hitting his shoulder, but she came equipped with a powerful temper. "Do you want the creepy man from across the street to stare at me?"

"What creepy man?" Brent stepped around her and headed for the window, peering out into the night. The apartments formed a U-shape, which allowed neighbors to spy on each other.

"Up there." Fontana pointed at a window that was shuttered. "Sometimes, he watches. Once I waved, but he didn't respond." She nervously adjusted her bangs.

"Did you tell management?" Brent noted the location of the apartment.

"No." Fontana shrugged. "I felt kind of stupid because he's not rude or anything. Just doesn't respond."

"Hmm." Brent looked at his watch. It was a bit late to knock at the door. "I'll be back in the morning. In the meantime, keep your door locked." He promptly climbed the ladder and installed the curtain.

"Now if I knew that playing my protector would've motivated you to complete the project, I would've tried that much sooner."

"Were you kidding me?"

"No. There is a man across the way that sits at the window." She handed him his jacket. "He's blind, though."

"Fontana, you're unbelievable."

"Whatever. You love me." She grinned.

Brent didn't deny the statement, although he wanted to wring her neck. Fontana was the youngest of his siblings and also the closest to him. Outside the immediate family, they had a long line of uncles, aunts and cousins that kept them busy at the obligatory family reunions and celebrations. Only within the past year had he started putting in an appearance at those family gatherings.

Two years ago, his wife's death had shattered his entire world. His grief swallowed everything in its path, seemingly without an end. He viewed everything around him with anger, pushing aside his family—especially his older brother.

Fontana tried logic. His pain seared deep within every part of him, making it difficult to listen to her counsel. Together with his mother's constant and sometimes brutal nagging, they'd managed to insert a crack into the wall he'd erected against the world.

He'd argued with Marjorie before she headed out for that late-night drive. An idiot with three DUIs on his driving record, combined with the worst possible timing, plucked his wife from his life.

The seedling of the idea to start an entertainment agency had been hers. Quitting would be giving up on her contribution. At times, forging ahead alone left him feeling adrift—with nothing and no one to anchor him.

"Good luck tomorrow. Let me know how it goes." Fontana kissed his cheek.

"Thank you, sis."

"You can always go back to law. Go back to pulling in tons of cash without all this drama."

"And you can always go back to college and get your degree," he remarked over his shoulder in the hallway.

Her front door clicked shut. Brent chuckled. They had butted heads over her early withdrawal from Boston University. None of his lessons on life moved her to change her mind. She wanted to pursue her acting career, and that was all she cared to do.

Yet he couldn't pretend not to understand her passion to pursue a dream. Look at him. He'd left a robust legal career to start his own entertainment agency. Managing the careers of various up-and-coming artists in the past year had solidified his determination to pursue this calling. His legal background served as an added bonus to his clients.

Although he had a strong, young team working in his agency, there was a missing component. No overhead existed for a robust public relations unit. After a few more years under his belt, the business could expand to have an in-house section. Right now, contracting out that portion of the business made sense.

The exercise of picking the right company caused him heartburn. Many of the potential firms didn't impress him or didn't gel with his vision for the latest R & B group he'd signed.

He really hoped that he didn't act too rashly over Charisse Sanford. Being desperate might cause him to be impulsive, but time was running out. He needed results from a solid public relations plan, as soon as possible. The label execs wanted to see numbers and not hear any excuses.

By midnight, the upcoming meeting remained on his mind. He rolled over, fluffed his pillows under his head and tried desperately to fall asleep.

"Charisse Sanford, I hope there's something substantive behind that sexy voice."

He shut his eyes, praying for good things to happen the next day.

Chapter 2

Charisse hovered in front of the Cuban restaurant, a tad unsure whether she should wait inside or meet Brent Thatcher outside. She didn't want to look eager, or as if she'd been stood up by her date. A quick glance at her reflection reassured her that she hadn't gone too evening dress with her attire.

The spring evening carried a slight cool edge. At least the weeklong streak of rain showers had ended last night. The city appeared clean and shiny, with a variety of muted and harsh lights from the various buildings spilling onto the sidewalks.

Charisse looked down at her black Betsey Johnson pumps. She deliberately chose the three-inch heels for that vertical boost. The rest of her outfit belonged in the high-end side of her closet. Her small selection of clothes had been handpicked to impress and elicit the right reaction to whatever she requested. Tonight's request was to be hired on the spot.

She absorbed the power from her straight cut, off-black Yves Saint Laurent pantsuit. Minimal embellishments and simple lines suited her style. Against the dark color, she wore a softly draped Donna Karan silk blouse with a hint of pink. Layered faux pearl necklaces with matching earrings and a bracelet from her favorite outlet store completed the ensemble. Her fingers were crossed that her investment had merit.

"Please do not let this be a no-show," Charisse muttered under her breath. Luisa had already assured her that no one had entered the restaurant asking for her.

Taxis pulled up and deposited their passengers. No one looked as if they were waiting for someone. She glanced at her watch, inwardly groaning that it was only five minutes past the hour. A black town car slowed and stopped at the curb, not an unusual sight in the city. Yet she kept her eye on the driver who emerged and walked around to open the rear passenger door.

Standing a head taller than the driver, the passenger stepped onto the sidewalk, adjusting his clothes. He'd be considered casually dressed against the starched uniformed driver and sparkling black sedan. But then again, the sight of an underdressed celebrity or businessman in the city wasn't rare.

The man glanced at his watch and then looked at the entrance of the restaurant. His gaze swept over and paused. Should she approach him? Before her mind and body collaborated, he headed her way.

Only a few feet separated him from her. In that short distance, she took in the confident, smooth gait that had a decided swagger. Each step had purpose to match the determined look of its owner. Up close, she noted the tailored silhouette of his pants, the matching black collared shirt. His physique was toned under the tailored clothing.

Nerves tingled.

Their eyes locked. She didn't move as he planted himself squarely in front of her.

With a subtle raise of his eyebrow, an upward tilt at the corner of his mouth, his hand extended toward her. "Charisse Sanford?"

"That would be me." Even in person, his husky tone melted over and through her. She shook his hand, trying to focus on the mouth that produced such a sexy voice.

"Brent Thatcher. Good to meet you."

"Call me Charisse." She disengaged her hand and headed to the restaurant's entrance. "Shall we?" She stepped aside for him to enter. Glad to see that he wasn't bothered by her holding the door for him.

He nodded and proceeded ahead but then stopped.

"Is something wrong?" Charisse asked. She stepped to his side for a better view of what caused such a reaction.

"I can tell that I'm going to like this place. Food smells good." He sniffed the air, and a slow smile spread across his face, lightening the mood. "I'm starved. A good meal is always the start of a great business relationship."

Charisse responded with a smile, grateful for the way he eased the tension. Right now she felt like she was taking a colleague out to dinner, rather than facing a critical job interview.

Could he look more handsome? The man was both suave and downright gorgeous. Her penchant for a man's mouth and eyes was already putting her in danger of being caught staring.

Thankfully, Luisa stepped up and greeted them.

"Welcome to Luisa's Cuban Cuisine. Señorita Sanford, always a pleasure to have you here."

"Thank you, Luisa. Tonight it's two. Quiet place, if possible."

"I'm sure that I can accommodate you."

They followed Luisa through the crowded restaurant into the rear. She walked past two rooms designated for smaller group dining.

She didn't want to think about how Luisa had managed to have a vacant room. She'd owe her friend a big favor for this.

"You've certainly got an impressive array of patrons," Brent remarked.

Charisse followed his gaze to framed black-and-white photos lining the wall.

"Yes, sir, we do have our share of celebrities and New York officials."

"Great endorsement. I must tell my friends about this place. I think I'm falling for it already," he replied.

"Appreciated." Luisa smiled and ushered them into the private room.

"Not that I think your opinion will change but you haven't even tasted the food," Charisse teased. Did his cocky swagger go along with an apparent decisiveness?

"Doesn't take long to recognize a good thing. And time matters to me."

Despite his husky, charming voice, she detected a steely, matter-of-fact tone to his delivery. She'd much rather be on the winning side of that voice.

Wasting Brent's time wasn't an option. However, he

was now on her turf. In this short time, she intended
to work her strengths, slide any shortcomings out of
sight and impress the heck out of him for the ultimate
goal—a contract. Although she could have met him in
the more casual dining area, she wanted the intimate
VIP room to highlight her connections to the who's who
of New York City.

Luisa pulled out a chair from the conference-style
table. "This is one of our small conference lounges."

A young man barely out of high school stepped into
the room.

"And this is your waiter. He'll attend to you this evening. If you should need anything further, don't hesitate
to ask. Enjoy and have a nice evening."

Charisse and Brent thanked Luisa. She added a wink
and small nod to her friend for the VIP rollout.

"Shall we?" Charisse motioned to the chairs that
were positioned at the middle of the table, opposite each
other. She waited for him to take his seat before she
pulled up to the table in her chair. Thank goodness, she
only had to interview with him and no one else. The
extensive length of the table and their positions opposite each other added a touch of formality to the event.

Charisse glanced over the oversize menu before
snapping it closed. She already knew her order. Very
rarely did she deviate from her favorite choice of *pollo
picante* with a salad. She'd hold on the beans and rice
since her nervous stomach had more than its fair share
to deal with.

"You know what you're getting, already?" she asked,
chancing a glance at his profile.

"I'm getting what you're having. Figured you know
what's good on the menu."

"So you'll go for the spicy grilled chicken?"

He nodded.

"And salad?"

He smiled. "Well, there I may have to step away from your lead and get a plate of fried sweet plantains."

Charisse nodded. "Now that's an excellent choice." Perfection seemed to have hit this man one wave after another. Not an ounce of excess fat lay visible on his face. The lean contour included a square jawline, a long narrow nose and eyes with the thickest eyelashes. She bit back her jealousy that he had what she had to get from a mascara wand. His eyebrows were equally thick, like bold accents to an already fabulous face.

The only question she had about his features was whether the unique shade of his eyes belonged in the gray scheme or soft blue. But she feared that if she stared any longer, she'd lose all sense of propriety. This was a business meeting, after all.

They submitted their orders and sat back comfortably.

"I'm glad that I have this opportunity to talk to you. I really figured that the job had been filled." She'd waited three months for a response from him, and there was always the ever-present worry that potential business wouldn't come to fruition.

"I'm taking my time. You know, being careful. The PR specialist will be working closely with me. Has to be someone I can trust and who can get up and running fairly quickly."

"Oh." Charisse imagined herself at his side, rolling up her sleeves to work. Suddenly her throat felt dry.

"And you have what I need. The PR campaign you launched for Dynamic Systems, the software company, last year impressed me. They managed to gain significant U.S. market share, a credit to your leadership. And Athletic One, the unknown athletic wear company sponsoring the tennis open, was genius. Again, you led the team." Brent raised his cup in a toast.

Charisse liked what she heard. He'd done his homework. Thankfully, she had several projects that had successful runs to prove that she knew what she was doing.

"Why did you leave? Seems like you had everything." Brent took a sip of water and set down the cup. His intense gaze zeroed in on her.

"That's true. Some days I do wonder why I opted to fly solo." Charisse shrugged. She resisted the urge to squirm. No need for the naked truth about her obsessive desire to be a successful businesswoman. "My dream had always been to have my own business in public relations. I did the prerequisite work with highly reputable companies for the experience. Now I'm building my clientele to a manageable level."

"I can get with that. Will I be able to meet your partner?"

"Ah…yes. Soon." Now, she did squirm. "She's on another project." Charisse nodded, offering a wide smile to distract him from further questions. She'd forgotten that she had mentioned Shelby's role in the management structure.

The waiter entered the room with a wide tray carrying their meals. Charisse exhaled and sank back in the chair, grateful for a break from Brent's questions. She'd rather eat and admire his lean face. Instead, she had to think ahead and stay alert for any loaded questions that could throw her off course.

"Let's eat." Brent grinned. His knife and fork were poised over his plate of spicy chicken.

"You don't have to tell me twice," she remarked, already cutting the tender meat.

Easy silence settled over the room as they savored the tasty meal. Even the waiter's checking in with them didn't generate much conversation.

"I can't believe I ate almost half the meal without looking up." Brent shook his head.

"I know what you mean. The food is spectacular. I find that conversation tends to interfere with the enjoyment."

"Thank you for making such an excellent choice." He raised his glass of wine.

"You're quite welcome." She warmed under his compliment. His easy and friendly attitude provided a certain level of comfort. She asked, "What made you strike out in this field? I'm sure the income for an entertainment attorney was substantial."

"I look at my background as a good foundation for doing something that is a labor of love. I love working with groups or individuals who have the talent and passion but don't have the good fortune to be connected with the right people. Getting your name out there is crucial in the business, especially when competition is huge and record companies only want to put out money on a sure thing."

"It is a brutal world out there," she agreed.

They continued to brief each other on their aspirations, along with challenges of the business. Charisse soon forgot that she was in an interview as she worked her way deeper into Brent's story.

"I'm enjoying your company. Let's have dessert,

so I can continue talking to you." Brent looked over the menu.

"Sure."

"Let's make a deal." He pointed at the desserts. "Why don't we share? I'm a tad full and only have space for a spoon or two of something decadent."

"Your pick."

She was pleasantly surprised by how informal he was—his easy conversation and suggestion to split dessert only increased her desire to work with him.

Brent looked up at her. "How about the Cuban banana custard tart?"

"Great. I was looking at that one, too." Brent snapped close the menu. "I think Luisa may be seeing me a little more often than she thought."

"That would be good. I love converting folks into fans of her food. You should also spread the word."

"I'm sure we'll be providing her with lots of business."

"Really?"

Brent nodded. "I've made up my mind. I want you to work with the guys. New Vision sounds like the perfect match. And you're someone I could work with."

Charisse rubbed her palms along her pant legs. Just like that, she had a job offer? Her pulse increased. Her excitement bubbled below the surface, aching for her to release it with a hoot and holler around the lounge. Luisa's kindness had produced remarkable results. They would have to celebrate later.

Once the Cuban banana custard tart was between them, Charisse waited for Brent to take the first bite. She knew what to expect from the creamy custard and the sweet banana. Besides, she did feel a bit shy about touching spoons with a man whom she barely knew.

Conversation over the dessert stayed on safe ground about the city and its diverse population.

"I've got to get back on the road. I'm glad that I went with my gut and met with you sooner than later. I'll have my secretary follow up with you. Charisse Sanford, it's been a pleasure."

Charisse shook his hand. There it was again. She'd dismissed it the first time, but now she was certain. Her body acted like a high school teen with an instant reaction. More than a tad embarrassed, she concentrated on hiding any overt feelings for his touch. The problem was that the tingling in her nervous system wasn't unpleasant.

"I look forward to working with you, Brent. I'm confident that you won't be disappointed."

"Your clients have certainly validated that statement."

Charisse sipped on the green tea to hide her shock. He'd already done a reference check. He came prepared, more so than she'd expected.

"I'll be traveling between New York and Boston. But I'm available by a number of means."

"That's not a problem." She loved the fact that he wasn't around to be a pain…or a distraction. Much about the man and his personality already proved to be murder on her thoughts.

Chapter 3

Since opening her own office, Charisse didn't need an alarm clock to start her day. She usually went to bed at night with her company's survival on her mind.

The morning routine started with her at the gym, sifting through her appointments while jogging at a Level Five incline. But today, she skipped the gym and headed to her office, ready to prepare for the new contract with Thatcher Entertainment Agency.

She switched on the lights throughout the small work area. The last song on the car radio still buzzed in her head. Before long, she was whistling the refrain while pulling out the coffee and filter to brew a fresh batch.

"Okay, this is new. I'm the one who makes the coffee. And what's with the whistling? Makes me wonder what you did last night." Tracy entered the kitchenette and shooed Charisse away. "Go to your office, I'll bring in the coffee when it's ready."

"I'm capable of making coffee."

"Not from what I've tasted." Tracy plucked the filter out of her hand and placed it in the coffee basket.

"Fine." Charisse headed to her office. She resumed her whistling even louder but broke into laughter when Tracy loudly protested.

A few minutes later, Tracy entered her office with two steaming coffee mugs. She had to navigate the strewn files on the floor, and she moaned with displeasure.

Charisse reached for her flowered mug and took a careful sip.

"What's happening here?" Tracy perched herself on the edge of the desk. Her frown deepened as she surveyed the room.

"I need to be better organized." Charisse looked up at her assistant. "You're not helping me in that department."

"That's because you're a lost cause, and you have a tendency to forget what I've told you to do."

"Would you give me a second chance?"

Tracy's mouth opened but then closed. Her eyes narrowed with a suspicious glint.

"I'm worth a second chance, if you ask my opinion. Plus I don't fancy having to train someone else to work on my new project."

"Wait! Oh, my gosh, did you get the project? You aren't kidding me?" Tracy waited for Charisse's nod before setting down her mug to do a happy dance around the table.

"Brent Thatcher is New Vision's newest client. I was a busy bee last night being interviewed. My credentials coupled with Luisa's delicious food provided the slam dunk to close the deal. The contract should be arriving today, unless Brent is just a smooth-talker. My gut says that he's a straight-up kind of guy."

"I want to meet this Brent. You know I have to approve of him. I'll be able to tell if he's worth anything."

"Trust me, the man is worth this and a whole lot more. He looks like the real deal. Seems pretty cool headed, but you can tell he's a shark. Something in those eyes." She tried to erase her smile. Maybe she shouldn't have mentioned his eyes, those grey-blue gorgeous eyes.

"Uh-oh. I don't like that look. That smile is scaring me." Tracy leaned down toward her face. "Are you excited because of the man or the project?"

"I know I'm acting silly, but I've got my head on straight." Charisse hoped that her cheeks wouldn't break into an idiotic smile. "Did you read the job spec? It's the perfect size account for me to cut my teeth. And there are even more opportunities that can come from it."

"Yeah, I read it. Looks interesting. We haven't worked with the entertainment field."

"We did work with that fashion designer."

"That is *so* not the same thing."

"You're stomping on my joy." Charisse didn't need Tracy to remind her that she was about to enter uncharted waters. But when had taking a unique path ever stopped her?

"Sorry." Tracy raised her hands in surrender. "Old habits. I like being safe and staying between the lines."

"Sometimes you have to push against the norm."

"That's why you're the boss. And I need to get

to work." Tracy picked up files from the outbox on the desk.

Charisse bit her lip to stop from asking the tough question. She swallowed the rise of her emotion that had the power to overpower logic.

"I think that I should still go to that interview on Friday." Tracy hung her head. "Look, I promise that I won't make any hasty decisions." She retreated toward the doorway.

"They'll love you on the spot. Even though the job market is tight, an employer knows when they have a good thing right in front of them. I can't blame them when they do."

"We'll see."

Charisse nodded, but the fact still remained that she needed not only Brent's contract but a few more mid-size contracts to feel comfortable. Without Tracy to assist her, managing additional clients would be labor intensive, as well as overwhelming. No one had to know just how difficult it could be. Somehow, she'd get through each obstacle. When it came to replacing Tracy, the obstacle would be one of her toughest.

No denying that they'd come through a lot together. Charisse relied on the young woman for almost everything. Working without her had never entered her mind.

Charisse sighed. Unlike Tracy, no child depended on her. Actually, no one waited at home. And she had deliberately taken that path as a way to reach her goal.

"We're cool?" Tracy's face reflected her concern.

"Of course." Charisse gave a thumbs-up. "I'm a big girl. I may pout, but I'm not hating. You don't need to add me to your list of people giving you grief." She held no resentment against this recent development. Tracy had managed to sneak past the barrier and settle in the emotional space between her heart and mind.

"That's what I love about you. Now back to work or whatever you're doing down there." Tracy blinked away her tears and headed out of her office.

"I'll miss you," Charisse whispered to the empty doorway.

She stacked the files that needed to be relabeled. The sounds of the office coming to life comforted her. Right outside her office, Tracy could be heard turning on her computer and then pulling out her work for the morning.

Jo, the receptionist, had arrived in a boisterous bustle as she bumped into every piece of furniture in her area. Her apologies and muttered curses flitted through the office. No matter how much she'd been talked to and how much she'd promised, Jo couldn't get herself into the office on time. Yet she worked hard for the small pay.

Lance, the fourth staff member, was hired to be Shelby's assistant. He was on vacation for a week. Charisse wouldn't be surprised if he came back to turn in his resignation. The workload was only sufficient for a part-timer. Lance looked bored most days.

"What the heck am I doing?" Charisse set aside the last file and then lay back on the carpet. Even though her office didn't have a fantastic view, she did appreciate the ceiling's skylight.

New York City sounds were nonstop, with sirens blaring, angry car horns sounding and the frequent assault of voices raising. With that colorful soundtrack, she gazed at the skylight, watching the pigeons perch and the clouds drift beyond her sight.

Nine months ago, she'd signed a year lease for the building that had finally opened six months later. She had no illusions that her business was going to take off. However, she also hadn't prepared for the administrative issues that had the power to bog down her business.

She didn't want to move from her spot on the carpeted floor. Instead, she crossed her legs, swinging her feet to the same tune she'd whistled earlier, which was now stuck firmly in her head.

From her vantage point, she added two things to her wish list: for Tracy to appear in her office with Thatcher's contract and to get the funds to paint her office. The institutional off-white color dragged on her mood. The first wish was a necessity. The second one was a nice option to pursue. Her thoughts drifted to delightful fantasies of what could be accomplished with some surplus money.

"Is this like a morning ritual? Should I join you?" asked Brent Thatcher, as he entered her office.

Charisse knew that if she was a cat, she'd have bounced straight up to the ceiling and hung on with her claws firmly implanted. Since she wasn't a cat, she only managed the undignified response of rolling over to her knees and pushing herself up.

"Didn't mean to startle you. But I did call out to you."

"You're here," she croaked. Not exactly her first wish but she'd accept this offering. She tried to think and move at the same time. "Why are you here?"

For Pete's sake, he could see her bare feet. She adjusted her clothes. Why didn't he quit grinning?

Her face warmed as her doubts tumbled over what he

may have seen, what he might think and why on earth she had decided to lie on the floor.

She zeroed in on her office door. She'd kill Jo and Tracy.

"By the way, Tracy told me you were in your office. I told her not to bother you," Brent piped up.

"Sorry, I wasn't expecting you." She brushed her clothes. Good thing that she had picked pants instead of a skirt. Her hair felt like it had exploded around her head into a mussed Afro. She needed a comb and a mirror, fast.

"My business kept me here overnight." Brent looked around the office, his eyes straying over her disorganized desk, then down to the open file drawers. "I wanted to see you in your digs. Hope you don't mind." He took a seat.

"Not at all." Charisse didn't like feeling as though she was in the passenger seat of her own car.

"You should've received the contract. If you've any concerns, I'm right here. Not to put any pressure on you, but I think we should get to work as soon as possible."

As Brent talked, Charisse brought up her emails. Sure enough, she had an unread message from someone in Brent's company. She opened the email and saved the contract in the Thatcher portfolio that she'd created for this moment.

"I'll need time to read this." She didn't know how many pages were in the contract, but it was sizable enough that she knew better than to sign it without an attorney reviewing it.

Although Brent was the picture of a sharp business-man in a steel-gray suit, crisp white shirt and navy blue tie, she wouldn't let his exterior be a distraction. She was determined to maintain a critical eye on everything.

"Sure, sure. I'll wait." Brent leaned forward on the desk and grinned.

That mouth did something to her senses. She followed his visual gaze around her office. His open survey of the area didn't bother her, until he paused at the photos on the credenza behind her. She fought the urge to look over her shoulder.

She had a photo with her parents at their last anniversary party. Another photo was of her college friends on their postgraduation trip to Cozumel. The third photo was still there out of habit. She'd broken up with Todd a while ago, but they were still friends. He'd moved south, back to his family's business. He'd rather work on his legacy than wait in the wings as she strived to create hers.

She couldn't read Brent's expression as he went from photo to photo.

Were her personal photos more important to him than the awards on the walls?

"Your daughter?"

"Excuse me?" She followed his gesture to the photo on her desk. "No. She's my niece."

"Ah. She's a pretty girl. Kind of resembles you. But I noticed the guy, over there. I assumed..."

"That's a friend. My niece is a sweetheart. I went with my brother's family to Florida and hung out at Universal Studios and Sea World last year."

"Do people mistake her for your daughter? It's uncanny how your features resemble each other."

"Yes. I get that a lot. I guess my family has strong

genes. How about you?" Her curiosity stood on heightened alert.

"I have strong genes, too." He laughed.

She waited to see if he'd talk about his marital state, but he didn't continue. Although sometimes she did push boundaries she wasn't about to do so with that subject. His naked ring finger didn't mean anything.

One thing was clear; she didn't know a lot about Brent. The conversation during her interview had been spent extracting information from her and not from him.

"Brent, I appreciate your eagerness to begin. Gives me confidence." She tried to think of a way to be diplomatic. "I will need time with the contract."

Tracy appeared in the doorway. Only after Charisse looked at her did she approach her desk.

"I know how busy you are. I'll give the contract a first read." Tracy retrieved the papers from her hand.

"Thank you."

Tracy walked out without another word. She didn't even look over at Brent. What happened to the first impression test she was supposed to do to clients? They hadn't discussed the signal for if Brent passed her first impression.

"Is that your assistant? She's quite efficient. Personally I think she'd be great as an investigator for captured terrorists. Getting past her was like a stealth mission balanced with diplomatic negotiations."

"She's a gem."

Tracy barely looked over her shoulder as she exited the office. Yet, Charisse didn't miss the small lift of a smile. Brent may have thought he'd scored a coup in using his charm to get past Tracy. Little did he know that Tracy didn't allow for anything accidental to happen.

"While Tracy takes care of the contract, I say we share guidelines. Do you have anything else up for discussion?"

"One client from your former agency said I'd be a fool if I didn't work with you."

"That was very nice of them. And I agree."

"Loyalty always impresses me. She had only nice things to say about you. Truly wished that she wasn't contractually tied up or she'd be on your roster."

"I never want or plan to raid my former employer's clients. It's a small world out there. And I do believe in karma."

"Commendable. But there may come a time when you both want the same client. What then?"

"I'll deal with that when it happens." Charisse wasn't close to competing with the big dogs. But that didn't mean she couldn't dream.

Brent was still a stranger, and even though he looked good, smelled better and dressed well, she wasn't about to roll over and share her inner thoughts.

"Not pushing you to make your decision. I have a, sort of, unusual request." Brent paused. "When I return in a few days, do you think that I can borrow a desk? I have an office downtown, but I'm willing to work in close quarters to brainstorm and ensure that things are starting off as planned."

Charisse hesitated. This man moved with an air to the unconventional, and she wanted to demonstrate her ability to adapt and be innovative. "That's not a problem. I do have a small office down the hall. It's available right now."

"You know, I like how you stay calm. Nothing seems to faze you. I just might make that my goal." He grinned.

"Um…Charisse, it looks like you have to meet with Takahashi in thirty minutes." Tracy said, as she burst into the office. "You won't make it across town. I'll call and let them know you'll be a few minutes late. Then this afternoon, you'll be at the studio with the McGuire Brothers." Tracy looked at Brent. Obviously the man lived to be offbeat. "Should I add anything else to your schedule?"

"Yes," Brent said, turning to Tracy. But whatever he was about to say turned into a tight lip at Tracy's glare.

Charisse almost giggled. This was why she needed Tracy. They were the perfect team.

"I'll give you time with your assistant. Think I'll go hunt down coffee."

"Down the hall." Tracy pointed down to the other end of the hallway.

Charisse waited until Brent had walked away before she motioned for Tracy to close the door. Her assistant was too happy to comply.

"Spill. You didn't tell me that he was freaking gorgeous. What the heck? I tell you when I see a cute dude. I sometimes even show you their photos on my phone. But when you expect the same consideration, your boss plays greedy. But anyway, I liked giving him a hard time."

"Now stop exaggerating before he hears you." Charisse looked over Tracy's shoulder at the closed door. "Plus no flirting with the clients. So save your undercover sex kitten–librarian look for someone else."

"I get it. Hands off."

"It's not like that." Charisse refused to allow her thoughts to meander in that direction. "Go call Takahashi, and leave me alone."

"I've got some good news on the contract."

"That was fast."

"An ex-boyfriend who is the in-house counsel for an insurance company came in handy."

"Look who's being resourceful. Did he make it back on your good side?"

"Ah, no. Nice guy but no spark where a spark was necessary."

"I know what you mean. Sparks should never be taken for granted."

"My ex says that the contract looks good. Not overly generous but not bad, either. He thinks you have room to negotiate on a few points. Here is his number if you want to chat."

"Definitely." Charisse took the number and placed it in front of her.

"I'll buy you some time with Takahashi. I'll make it an hour. You need to close this deal. So don't waffle. Call that number now." Tracy headed for the door. "In the meantime, I'll go see how our new client likes his coffee."

Charisse nodded. Brent had passed muster with Tracy. She felt much better and picked up the phone.

Tracy's ex proved to be a wealth of information. In fifteen minutes, she had the clauses circled and her objections noted. Now she had to turn on the businesswoman skills.

A knock on the door interrupted her. She slid the contract off the table and into her drawer. It was time to slip into the driver's seat.

"Come in." She knew it was Brent.

"Ready for me?"

"Actually I've gone over the contract, and I'm ready to discuss a couple things."

"Fire away."

"Given your longer-term plans, I recommend that the terms be twelve months. Anything less is handcuffing me and doing your client a disservice."

"Got it."

"I want to be able to use my own team or have the freedom to choose."

"But I have experts, too."

"I'm sure you do." Charisse held her tongue and waited. If he had all the experts, he wouldn't have needed her.

"Got it."

"I've given you my fees and schedule of payments. Anything outside of the scope of reasonable time and specified services needs mentioning."

"Got it."

Charisse took a deep breath. "I'll wait for a revised contract."

"Once that's done, can we start working?"

"We can discuss the schedule until the final version arrives."

Brent looked frustrated, but she wasn't budging. She didn't stop him when he excused himself and left her office. Instead, she pulled out the contract and looked at the first page with her handwritten notes. She'd never been fired from a job and hoped that this wasn't going to be a first.

"Your revised contract." Tracy stood in front of her holding a sheaf of papers.

"You're kidding me. That was fast."

Brent walked up behind Tracy. "I don't like to waste time. You'll notice that about me."

Charisse noticed a lot more about him than that. He carried a power that drew her attention and held it fast. If she wasn't careful, she would end up giving him her undivided attention. But she had a company to run and more contracts that needed to be won.

Would Brent prove to be a distraction of epic proportions?

"What's your day looking like now?" He took the contract from Tracy's hand and placed it in front of her. "Please sign, or else I know you won't answer me on anything."

"Is this how you got that R & B group? Nagged them into submission?" Charisse took the papers and skimmed through the document.

All her changes had been inserted in the latest version. Satisfied and relieved, she initialed each page and signed the last page.

Brent stepped up and signed the last page on the line opposite her name.

"Now if you don't mind, I'll take this from you so I can make copies and file them." Tracy took the contract.

"In my defense, I didn't nag anyone," Brent said. "I drove the group around and then took them to my mother's for dinner."

"My mother is a darn good cook herself," Charisse said. "But I never considered using her skills to make deals."

"Oh, really, well, we must put that to the test."

His voice stroked her skin. The mere thought of skin-to-skin contact with him caused a chain of goose bumps to pop up along her arms. She shifted in her seat and rubbed her arms.

His gaze was innocent. No sly wink or wry twist of the lips to serve as a teasing invitation. But she wasn't buying it. This man knew he was drop-dead gorgeous. Whether he wore casual off-the-rack clothes or his spiffy designer, custom-fitted fashion, he made a woman want to check herself in the mirror for his attention.

"My mother can cook, too." Tracy dropped the copies onto the desk.

Charisse jumped, and was glad to see that Brent did, too. The mood in her office needed to be zapped out of existence. And she didn't go after her attractive male clients. She certainly didn't pursue men who didn't share mutual feelings.

"Welcome, Brent, New Vision looks forward to working with you." Charisse offered her hand. "To a great partnership."

"I'm sure it will be."

"Charisse, you have to get going." Tracy tapped her watch.

"Are you available tomorrow evening? We can order takeout and hammer out the details before I fly back to Boston," Brent interrupted.

"Right." Charisse pushed back her chair. "Tomorrow evening…ah, I guess so."

Multitasking wasn't a strong point for her today. As she gathered up her briefcase, she wondered if this off-kilter feeling would diminish as she got used to Brent's style. Normally her feet stayed grounded, along with her head and heart.

"Great. Better go make your client happy. I won't keep you from your appointments. Thanks for accommodating my crazy schedule."

"Not a problem."

"Tracy, please make sure Brent is comfortably situated in the office."

Charisse didn't move until Tracy took up being the tour guide for Brent. They walked together down the hall as she gave him a quick tour of the essentials like the kitchen and restroom.

Tracy's voice faded, along with Brent's questions, which were occasionally interrupting the orientation.

"Time to get moving," Charisse said.

She gathered her scarf and light jacket. Her heels clicked on the wooden floor of the hallway. She had to pass Shelby's office—now Brent's—before heading to the reception area.

Would the bright sherbet yellows and chocolate mousse color scheme drive him to distraction? She would love to see him unsettled. The room was probably a fraction of the size of his own office. She imagined that he had a grand office with all the latest technological gizmos.

She slowed down as she approached the office, listening for Tracy's or Brent's voice. Instead it was quiet. She passed the doorway and saw him working on his laptop. Just as she thought he was about to look up, she hurried on her way.

Brent sat in the office and exhaled slowly. Tracy reminded him of a drill sergeant, a worthy addition to any well-run office. He recognized the connection between

Charisse and her. They obviously respected each other. Good vibes on a team were vital.

With the contract signed, work had to begin immediately. He didn't intend to come down heavy and desperate for her business, but he had the record company, production team, potential sponsors and eager family waiting for the guys to ignite. Unfortunately, these days they didn't wait terribly long for an act to catch on. He may be confident in Charisse's abilities, but the reality was that he was on a short leash.

Tomorrow night he'd head back to Boston to work on getting the group to New York. The city might be brutal for new arrivals to the music scene, but it was the place to prove themselves.

With the right planning and appearances at targeted venues, the guys could be a surprise hit. He sent a message to his secretary to work on the travel arrangements.

An email popped up from one of his partners. It was a harried message about a new artist under their consideration. Another agency had just stepped into the mix and flown her to New York. The problem was that she hadn't committed to his firm.

"Darn it!" He pinched the bridge of his nose in frustration.

He wanted to unearth the diamond beneath her gruff exterior. With her gritty style and powerful voice, she would give the hot acts a run. Bottom line, he wanted her signed with his agency.

Every client who came into Thatcher Entertainment had been vetted by him. He had a brand to build and protect not only for himself but also for his clientele.

"Vicki, get in touch with Leila. Let her know that

I'm in the city. I want to meet with her, as soon as possible." He waited for his secretary to take notes. "Don't take no for an answer."

He answered several more emails. If he didn't keep up with the volume, the deluge could take up most of his day.

A few minutes later, his phone buzzed. He snatched it up.

"Yes, Vicki." He listened to his secretary give him the news he'd hoped she get. "Tell her that I'm on my way. Now get reservations at the Club. Thanks."

He took a deep breath and then started shutting down his laptop. His schedule had now taken a sharp detour. As long as he was back this evening to work with Charisse, he'd be satisfied.

A flash of color out of the corner of his eye startled him. He turned toward the doorway. Someone who he was sure was Charisse whisked past the door. He grabbed his briefcase to follow, hoping that he wasn't mistaken.

Brent didn't make it to the elevator in time. He stabbed at the elevator button. The numbers lit overhead with its slow progress to the first floor.

"Come on," he urged. He stabbed the button once more.

Finally the elevator arrived and the doors slid open. He almost pumped his fist that the cab was empty. Hopefully he'd have an express ride to the lobby.

As soon as the door opened wide enough for him to exit, he slid through with a noisy exit. The security guard looked up at him, but when he waved, the man returned to signing in a messenger.

Ahead he saw Charisse push against the revolving

door, heading onto the street. He pulled out his cell phone and made a call to his driver. If he was lucky, his timing wouldn't be off.

Several taxis whizzed past Charisse. Looked like the New York cab system would help with his impromptu plan. By the third pass, she lowered her hand to her hip. He strode onto the street in time to see her mouth tighten in anger.

Sexy.

"Since I know I'm the culprit for making you late, the least I can do is give you a ride to your next appointment," Brent said as he strode over to her.

She had already stepped out into the street with both hands raised as if to forcibly stop the next taxi.

"Good grief, you just scared me." Charisse turned her attention from the street. Her hand gripped her blouse over her heart.

"Well you should get out of the street before one of these crazy drivers make you into roadkill."

"I don't have time for this," Charisse said.

"Okay, you stand on this sidewalk, and I promise to get you to your appointment on time."

She looked at him as if he'd said something strange. Her head tilted to the side, and she furrowed her brow. Finally, the sound of an angry horn made her hop to where he stood.

Standing shoulder to shoulder, with her hair whipping, her soft fragrance drifted in the air with a light, floral scent.

"I'll take that offer."

Brent motioned to his driver who had hung back until he signaled.

"Here, allow me." He pulled a piece of torn paper from her hair.

Her dark brown hair always had a healthy sheen to its thick body. His fingers lingered over the silky strands. Unbidden thoughts of his hands sliding through her hair, cupping her head, slammed into his consciousness. He withdrew his hand and even took a step back for good measure.

"Thanks. That would have been embarrassing."

He nodded, fighting his body's reaction to her proximity. He hoped that she sat all the way near the other passenger door. Instant attraction didn't sit well with him. He didn't believe in it—not since Marjorie. Moving on with the business was hard enough.

Charisse followed his driver's prompt to enter the car. She slid across the seat to the far end, as he'd hoped. He stayed close to the door near him. Within the confines of the car, her fragrance played havoc with his concentration. He adjusted his tie before playing with the knobs for the air-conditioning panel.

"I appreciate this. I'm heading to 33 John Street."

Brent nodded.

"Sorry, but I didn't have time to touch up my makeup." Charisse held up her compact.

Brent pretended that he didn't care. Yet he glanced at the deliberate movement of the lipstick gliding across her lower lip and then covering the top lip. His throat went dry. She smacked her lips together, and he almost groaned.

The toffee-brown shade suited her. The gloss in the color accentuated her bow-shaped mouth with full lips. His gaze didn't shift as she talked and continued retouching her makeup.

"Seems like a lot to do," he stated.

"I can feel you being critical." She glanced sideways.

"I'm fascinated, that's all."

"I know that I'm not the first woman you've seen put on makeup. As a matter of fact, I'm sure that you've seen your fair share."

"What's that supposed to mean?" He waited. "Now who's being critical?"

"Oh, come on. Good looks. Nice clothes. Fancy car. You could be a secret agent, for all I know." She resumed tending to her brows.

"That's not my style," he said slowly.

Something in his tone made her pause. She snapped her compact closed and put away her makeup.

"Sometimes you can't help what comes your way. While you try to play the choirboy, I'm sure women have you in their crosshairs."

"Then it sounds like I need to be rescued." Brent's gaze slid from her to the scenery outside the window.

The car jarred to a stop at a red light. The space narrowed between him and her. He cleared his throat and repositioned himself.

Thank goodness for the snap back to reality, he thought.

Charisse looked at him. Her hand stroked her throat, playing with the thin gold necklace. "I've been tossing around a few ideas for the guys." She tilted the air-conditioning vent toward her face.

"I'm listening."

"As soon as you have a single, I think we should have a series of press junkets and meet-and-greets in record stores."

"Okay," he nodded. "I don't want any of those tabloid types to dilute the press pool."

"Understood. They can be vicious. One or two of them aren't bad. If you get them on your side, they can be quite helpful."

"Can't risk it. You can't control the message."

"Why not? It's time to think outside the box," Charisse pushed.

"Now you're turning my words against me."

"I don't need to remind you how many boy bands are out there. The public is fickle. These guys have to come up with something different."

"And throwing them to the tabloids to get their image ripped apart is the answer?" Brent's temper flared.

"Not if you have connections." She pointed to herself. "Like me."

"It's risky." Brent had his roadmap for each artist down on paper. He ran his agency like he had run his law firm. Every step was part of a larger design.

"You need the teen girls to want to get to know these guys," Charisse said. "You want them to have momentum on Twitter and Facebook. I studied the DVDs you sent me. The group sounds good. They look good. They have all the ingredients to be a megasuccess, but no platform. Do they have what it takes to stick it out for the long haul?" she asked.

"Are you sure you want to direct that question at me?" He stared at her, hating the question, as well as the tone.

He locked his glare with her direct gaze, silently pushing against her doubts...his doubts.

"Looks like I've arrived at my destination." She gathered her pocketbook and briefcase.

Brent wanted to continue with his defense. He didn't think she had the wrong approach, but he wasn't sure that she was one-hundred-percent correct, either. Wasting time with the wrong strategy had consequences, especially with a record label involved.

The car slowed to a stop. The driver got out and walked around to Charisse's door.

"Relax. I like to play the devil's advocate. Brings perspective to the discussion." Charisse raised her eyebrow at him and scooted out of the car. "Thanks for the ride. See you tomorrow?"

Brent nodded. "Good luck with your meeting."

He waited until she entered the building before signaling to the driver to continue.

Tomorrow? She didn't have to say the word like a teasing invite. Maybe he didn't need to react to everything as if he'd never been around an attractive, business-savvy woman. And he didn't want her to play devil anything. All his research about her hadn't prepared him for this temptation.

Could he relax and allow her to run with her ideas? And did he have the grit to resist casual flirtation? That was the million-dollar question.

Chapter 4

Charisse wrapped up her meetings with Takahashi and the McGuire Brothers, grateful that these clients were completely on board with her suggestions. She had taken for granted having her clients take her advice without rebuttal. Brent's rejection of her ideas had stoked her anger, and his second-guessing had worked her nerves.

Freedom to create her ideas and plans was important. If Brent questioned her every move along the way, it would dampen her creativity.

Now she felt the need to prove her worth early on in the game. Instead of going to her hair appointment for a touch-up and trim, she rebooked and headed to someone she knew had good advice and contacts. The fact that he was also interested in her was an irritating factor, but she had always managed to hold him off.

Three cups of coffee later, Jake still hadn't shown

up. He wasn't known for his punctuality, but an hour late was beyond the bounds of her patience. He was a former colleague from a competing firm. They had worked together on some projects but for the most part, tended to be on opposite sides of the fence, vying for the same contracts.

Although he had a reputation with women, she didn't ever plan to be one of his conquered prizes. However, Jake had contacts that she needed and knowledge that could benefit her.

"Wipe that frown off that pretty face." Jake slid into the chair opposite hers. He unzipped his jacket but didn't remove it. His dark eyes sparkled with their usual mischievous glint.

"You're getting worse about the punctuality. I don't have much time."

"Much time for what? Now that you're the boss lady, you look uptight. I thought you'd be running around like a queen diva."

"Queen diva, oh, please. You've got the wrong woman."

"You're also cranky. Talk to Jake, let's see if I can turn that frown upside down." Jake added a cheesy grin. His little-boy looks didn't seem to match his supersize frame.

"You're lucky I'm desperate."

"Words that I've wanted to hear for so long."

"Stop." Charisse waved away the innuendo as she did with all of Jake's flirtatious comments.

"Okay, talk. By the way, in case you think that you're the only important person with your boutique office, I'm actually moving up the feeding chain myself." He raised his water glass.

"Congratulations, Jake. That's great. You are a PR guru, even if you're egotistical and sexist." Charisse clinked water glasses with him.

"Too many big words. But I'll take the compliment."

"I've got good news, too. I have a new client."

"Cheers." He took her coffee cup and took a long sip. "Ack. Not enough sugar." He signaled the waitress to bring another cup. "Tell me about your new income stream."

"Ex-lawyer turned manager of a new R & B group. He's looking for a PR campaign to get them a fan base and some exposure."

"Tricky. Is the group worth the effort?"

"I saw a video of them—talented, good-looking guys."

Jake shrugged. "With the right momentum, nowadays you can make anyone a star."

"That's the general feeling, but I still think that eventually the fans would get bored if there's nothing to back up the glitz." Charisse thought of all the one-hit groups that delivered a big bang but then fizzled on their sophomore attempts.

Jake tapped the table for her attention. "What do you need from me?"

"It's not really a problem yet. I mean, it's only been the first day that we chatted about the plans. Maybe I'm overreacting."

"I know this is our usual coffee meet up so I can bring you up-to-date on the industry gossip and goings-on. However, I am also your mentor." He raised his hand at her quick protest. "No need to be modest. You know you love my wisdom."

"He's not agreeing with me." Charisse rushed the admission to cut Jake's climb onto his soapbox.

"I can handle his stupidity a few ways. I can have a little talky-talk with him." He cracked his knuckles, grinning evilly at her.

"I think he could probably pulverize you." Charisse snorted.

Jake had the physique of a heavyweight boxer. But over the years, Charisse learned that he was a teddy bear with a soft spot for the ladies.

On the other hand, her latest client had to be over six feet tall, with several inches to spare. Where other men were tall and lanky, Brent had enough all-over muscular tone to set him apart. She'd seen his muscles flex and move beneath his clothing at dinner and in her office. But even more impressive than his physical assets was his inner grace, ease and sophistication. His emotions hid behind a handsome face that offered only an occasional glimpse of what lay beneath the surface.

"I'm a man who knows his limitations. I would be the king of diplomacy as I cut his legs from under him."

Charisse laughed. Jake certainly had earned that exact reputation with those who got on the wrong side of him. No need to go so hardcore with Brent, though.

She continued, "I want to know if I can get an introduction to the host for the local entertainment cable station."

"Gladys Beecher? I think I could do that. You know she wants me."

"Well, introduce me to her before you screw up that working relationship. I'll need that as soon as possible."

"How is she going to help you win over your new client?"

"He needs to see that I can deliver. And this would be a sizable present. Then I can have space for some of the other ideas I have in mind."

"He'd be a fool not to give you your space."

Charisse nodded.

"Well, if he still gives you a hard time…call me whenever, wherever, *bella.*"

"Not in a million years." Charisse rolled her eyes.

Jake shrugged. "Don't go falling for him."

"I'm not like you. I don't try to go horizontal on all my clients."

"You make me sound like I don't have discerning tastes. I'm keeping myself pure for you."

"Oh, I'm flattered. But don't ruin some woman's fantasy on my account." She drained her coffee. "Call me as soon as you've made contact with Gladys." She blew him a kiss.

"Stop toying with me. I'll let you know about Gladys. Now I have to go find a woman willing to buy me dinner."

Charisse laughed at Jake's woeful expression. She gathered up her pocketbook and stood. They hugged. She ignored Jake's groan and pushed him away.

Even though she had Jake in her corner helping nab Gladys, she didn't want to rely on that as her only major delivery. She placed another call to her contact at a music magazine who had a reputation for being friendly toward new acts.

Once she'd had time to think about what she wanted, she was more certain that she had a good publicity plan for the band.

The crisp spring day felt good. She decided to walk some of the way back to her office. After a fruitful day of appointments, she liked the solitude of strolling down the busy streets crammed with buildings and traffic. The mixture of the two worlds colliding energized her.

New York City had become her new home after she graduated from college and made the easy decision to leave her parent's home in upstate New York. She was a hometown girl, a homecoming queen destined to marry the high school quarterback. But her dreams had matured throughout college, and she had moved on, planting her feet squarely in the heart of New York City and working for other public relations firms for several years.

While she attended her friends' weddings and baby showers, she remained the odd one out—completely unattached, with no dependents. She tried to be interested in their daily lives, but she felt worlds apart from their domestic concerns. Her mother begged for her to stop running herself so ragged. But Charisse felt her mother had lived the cookie-cutter lifestyle for too long.

Charisse strolled past an art gallery with various artwork in the window. The small shop called out to her. The watercolors especially touched her as a reminder of her mother's creative dreams. A wave of homesickness washed over her.

"May I help you? I'm the owner." A smiling woman greeted her entry.

"Thank you, but I'm browsing."

"Take your time. We're also featuring an artist from Belize."

"Sounds interesting." Charisse followed the owner into a small alcove dedicated to the artist's works.

The owner smiled as she trailed her finger along a

frame. "This is my favorite. The artist painted an abstract that embodies the hope for Belize. You can see the people dancing and celebrating among the large fabric of the flag that unites them."

Charisse studied the artistry. Many points touched a chord with her own aspirations and struggles. She turned to the owner. "I'd like to savor the work."

"Of course." The gallery owner left her in the room.

Charisse had learned early from her mother to allow art the time to speak to its audience. She had seen the evidence when her mother pulled out her sketchbook and started drawing. Years later, she'd discovered tons of her mom's finished work.

That moment came back so vividly.

"Mom, you're good." Charisse held up the painting *of the town from a high point that was a lookout point for tourists.*

"With you and your brothers and sister gone, I have time now."

"Better hope Dad doesn't retire, then," Charisse joked.

"That's in the works."

"Really." Charisse sat opposite her mom, waiting for her to elaborate.

"Time for me to start my career."

"Oh." Charisse could've kicked herself for sounding judgmental.

"I know what you're thinking. I should be thinking about retirement time with your father. But this is what I agreed to do from the beginning when we became parents."

"That was a mighty long promise to hold."

Now that she had the opportunity to admire this artist's inspiration, Charisse could understand why her mother never stopped believing.

However, she didn't know where that faith came from to understand the depth of such a sacrifice. How would she learn? Looking at her naked fingers without so much as a friendship ring, she imagined that she'd first have to deal with her commitment issues.

She left the gallery store, promising to return. She'd love to make it a mother-daughter outing. She rarely had time to relax and be in the moment, and drifting through the small gallery had provided a comforting surge against her insecurities.

A text buzzed its arrival on Charisse's phone. It was Shelby, saying she would stop by the office tomorrow to chat.

She dialed Tracy. "Shelby is coming to the office tomorrow. Not sure what time. Please clear my schedule."

"Done. Wait a minute. What about Thatcher?"

Charisse sucked in air through gritted teeth. She didn't want to reschedule him.

"He's supposed to come in the evening. She should be gone by then," Charisse said.

"You're right. Would serve her right if she came to the office and he was sitting at her desk. Okay, we should be all set."

"Good luck."

Charisse hung up. Tomorrow was going to be a stress-filled day. First, she'd have to deal with Shelby. Then she'd have to deal with Brent.

Both people could affect her dream. She wanted to prepare for the worst with Shelby. With Brent, she planned to give him her best.

Thatcher Entertainment Agency, as part of her business portfolio, would help keep her focused on the big dream, a dream that may now have to unfold with only her at the helm of a small team. One task at a time, she'd prove to Brent that he'd made the right choice. Tomorrow he'd be back in her office with his infectious quirky personality. The man's charm had an addictive quality that left her wanting more of his attention. Worse, he made her want to be…sexy. His appreciation of her femininity wasn't lost on her.

She crossed the road, heading to her hairdresser. Her hair needed work. She splayed her fingers in front of her. The chipped polish on several nails made her wince. All she wanted to do was to look like the executive she was. That's all.

Two hours later, with dusk already settling over the city, Charisse emerged from the hairdresser with a new hairstyle. The decision to take off several inches came with a swiftness that even shocked her hairdresser. The last time she had worn her hair short was in college, and with the new feathered bob, she could again feel the breeze against her neck.

Her hand absently stroked the back of her neck. A small smile played across her face as she imagined how her friends would react to the new look. She headed back to the office with a new burst of energy, ready for another late night of work.

Her phone rang. She was afraid that it was Shelby. But this time it was Jake.

"What's up?"

"Good news. Gladys said to give her a call. She can't promise anything, but she'll at least give you face time."

Charisse wrote down the phone number.

"And before you thank me, I've got a solution to another problem."

"What problem?"

"Don't try to hide things from me. I know two-faced Shelby is supposed to be with you at New Vision. If you'd asked me, I'd have told you to move on without her."

"I'm not in the mood for a lecture. Go ahead with your news." Charisse suddenly felt tired. She was ready for a cab to take her straight home.

"I found an extra pair of hands for you."

"I am not working with you." The thought was outrageous.

Jake's laugh boomed over the phone.

Charisse didn't think it was funny, just a waste of her time. "I'm going to hang up."

"No, wait. I found someone, really. I'm not lying." Jake continued to chuckle. "An intern. Labor in exchange for work experience and college credit. You interested?"

Charisse balled her fist in triumph.

"You still there?" Jake asked.

"Yes. Jake, why are you being so helpful?"

"'Cause it's you."

"I owe you big—"

"And you're wondering about the repayment," Jake taunted.

"Kinda, yes."

"I genuinely like and respect you. I want to see you succeed and kick butt in this industry," Jake seriously.

"That's very noble."

"You don't sound like you believe me."

"Would you believe you?"

Jake laughed. "I guess you have a point. Really, our company is using this intern, and I got them to agree to share her with you."

"Wait a minute. I'm not sure I'm comfortable with that. It's a conflict of interest."

"Already thought of that. She's wrapping up her time with us. But I'm sure she could get an extension to work with you, until you have the time to hire someone."

"I'll think about it. Send her over."

"Great."

Charisse hung up, wondering if she was really being helped. But she didn't mind working with a student, since they usually worked hard.

Chapter 5

Brent headed for an after-party being hosted by the record label of one of his female artists. He normally didn't put such events on his calendar because he hated attending them. But since he was in New York and his artist's contract would be up in six months, he'd put in an appearance.

Parties bored him. No business was being discussed with loud music as a backdrop. Everyone attending appeared to have an agenda—to meet or nab someone in the music industry. His friends pushed him to get out more. But if this is what the dating scene had become, he'd happily stay home. What was the point, anyway?

Even in a noncommittal relationship, he'd have to open himself up. He had no desire to do so. Nor did he have the energy to nurture the various stages of a relationship—not to mention that he didn't know how to move on from Marjorie's passing two years ago.

No one, not even Charisse Sanford, could stir anything in him.

"Brent, good to see you."

He turned, subconsciously hoping it was Charisse's voice he heard.

"Brent, yoo-hoo." A woman standing near the registration table waved her hand madly at him.

"Hi, Francine. It's good to see you." He submitted to her kissing each of his cheeks. The woman wanted so badly to be British, and it was always painful to listen to her faux accent.

"Didn't know you were in town. I told you to look me up the next time you were here." She slid her hand between his arm and his body, then pressed her breast against his arm.

"I'm only popping in. I've got a busy day tomorrow, along with it being a long one." He attempted to extricate his arm, but her hand tightened.

"Have a drink with me?"

Brent nodded, but this time he peeled her fingers off his arm. The woman had a grip like a python. He headed for the bar. She didn't let him out of her sight as she stayed on his flank.

"Cheers." She toasted. "Why are you playing hard to get?" She wiggled her shoulders.

"It's not a game."

"I'd hope not." Her mouth shaped into a pout.

"Have you seen your father?" Brent had no intention of being caught up in Francine's crazy fantasies. Dealing with the record label and with her father, the CEO, made the situation particularly dicey.

"Daddy is here chatting it up with the European bigwigs. Brent, please dance with me." Francine threw up her hands and danced provocatively in front of him.

A female body that had been fine-tuned to perfection didn't escape unnoticed by him. That didn't mean that he didn't have discerning tastes when it came to actually socializing with the woman. If he could have a straightforward conversation with Francine, he'd be able to explain their incompatibility. Something was lacking in her, and it had nothing to do with her physical self.

He was more inclined to look for that inner beauty that seemed indefinable. Yet he could sense the quality, like he had when he was in Charisse's company on the first night they'd met.

"If you keep standing there like a statue, you'll make me think that you don't want to be with me." She tiptoed and leaned close to his ear. "You don't have to worry about daddy finding out." She blew into his ear.

Brent brushed his ear, more irritated than turned on.

"Francine, if you don't mind, I need to talk to Brent."

"Sure, Daddy." Francine slid herself off his body and walked away with her hips bouncing with ever more emphatic beats.

"Good to see you, Brent."

"Mr. Caldwell, how are you?" Brent could do without the hearty handshake and heavy arm around his shoulders. He didn't know if the welcome was business or personal.

"I'm a happy camper. We've got acts that are hitting the charts in their debut. Others have nabbed some key nominations. Your solo act, Tairelle, is gaining a fan base with the young women that's unbelievable."

Brent nodded.

"Not sure where your head is at, but we are pleased with the advance copies of the sample songs. The single collaboration with that Miami reggaeton group is soaring up the charts. All the clubs are playing it."

"All good news." Brent already knew the details of his artists. He made sure his team kept up with their progress, in case they had to make any quick adjustments.

"Got anyone else you want me to take a look at?"

"Maybe."

"Well, you know what to do." Caldwell smacked him on the shoulder and offered a curt nod.

Brent felt as if he should stand at attention and not move until Caldwell was out of sight. The man ran over anyone who didn't get out of his way fast.

"I'll let you get back to Francine." Caldwell grinned like a used-car salesman before heading back into the crowd.

The loud music kept rhythm with the pounding in Brent's head. This scene didn't mesh with his vibe. It was time to go.

The second that he emerged from the building, he took a deep breath. Over his shoulder, he took note of the various celebrities still arriving. Thankfully, his car arrived in time for his escape.

"Brent!"

"Darn it." Brent turned to see Francine hobbling her way to his car. Her giggling was a sure sign that she'd had too much to drink. He waited for what he knew was coming.

"I'm not letting you out of my sight." She pushed herself against his body.

Brent turned his head to avoid being imprinted by her bloodred lipstick.

"Let's go," she begged. "I can hardly wait for us to finally get into bed."

The idea of being with her triggered him into action. He held her firmly by the shoulders and pushed her away.

"I'm going to my hotel—alone. Let's end this on an amicable note."

Her eyes flashed from sleepy and provocative to cold diamonds of anger.

"You bastard! How dare you treat me like this?"

"Good night, Francine." Brent got into the car. Having an argument with her in her current state wouldn't do either one of them any good.

From his window, he read her lips as she cursed at him. A number of passersby stopped to gawk and openly laugh. Brent closed his eyes. He couldn't help but look forward to tomorrow evening, which he was sure would not have the drama of this night.

Charisse didn't mean to stay at work as late as she did. By the time she got home, took her shower and fell into bed, there were only a few more hours until her morning alarm clock would blare.

Normally she'd be ready to go and face the mountain of things to complete. Today was a bit different. Now she sat in her office sipping on coffee, waiting for the day to begin.

A knock on the door roused her.

"Do you have a life beyond these four walls?" Shelby asked, walking in.

"Didn't expect you quite so early." Charisse couldn't

help her mouth from opening to show how stunned she was. Shelby stood in her office in a black suit, posing as if she were at the end of a fashion runway. Her background in runway modeling was evident.

"Okay, now you're exaggerating. Why is my presence so shocking?"

Charisse shrugged. Her partner didn't need to make an appointment to talk to her or to visit the office. However, her reluctance in joining New Vision hadn't left Charisse with much confidence that it would ever be a reality.

"Hello, Shelby." Tracy popped her head into the office. "Sorry, I'm late, *boss.*"

Charisse waved away the apology.

"Will you be using your office, Shelby?" Tracy asked. The corner of her mouth lifted derisively.

Shelby shook her head. "I'll be gone soon after I speak with Charisse." She moved to the other side of the door and rested her hand on the knob.

Tracy didn't push. Like Charisse, she must have heard Shelby's very businesslike tone. She had barely left the doorway when Shelby closed the door.

So it was going to be like that. Charisse took a deep breath, readying herself for an encounter that was already making her stomach rumble nervously.

"The office looks great." Shelby flicked her hand in a way that showed off the sparkling bracelet at her wrist. "You've done a good job with the decorating. If I had the time, I would have brought in my decorating team. They owe me for the amount of work they've done in my house." She smiled, but the effort looked cold. "You haven't been to my parties."

"You didn't invite me."

"We're friends. Why on earth do you need an official invitation. *Mi casa es su casa.*"

Charisse sighed. She didn't want to dance around the issues, but obviously Shelby had such plans. The way she strolled around her office and offered lopsided smiles came across as if she were toying with her.

"Look, Shelby, I have to get busy. Work to do. Appointments to keep."

"I remember when you and I were the green ones in the office. We helped each other. We looked out for each other."

"And then you went your way."

Shelby nodded. She removed her glasses and bit the edge of the handle. "I sidestepped to climb that ladder."

"I know."

"And I haven't stopped climbing, Charisse."

Charisse noted Shelby's calm demeanor. She had always been quiet but deliberate. Today, however, there were subtle changes. Her fingers clenched and unclenched along the edge of her blouse. A soft blush that wasn't the product of makeup bloomed on her cheeks. A muted excitement burned in her eyes, stirring chills through Charisse.

"I've started my own company."

"What?" Charisse snapped the rubber band that she'd worked around her fingers, disregarding the slight sting of the band popping.

"I landed that big contract at my company. Then it hit me—kind of the way your *it* moment suddenly hit you."

"It didn't *suddenly* hit me." Charisse tried to sound rational, despite her raging thoughts. "My goal has always been to have my own company."

"Anyway, I figured that you'd set this up." Shelby shrugged. "This is your place, your dream." She sniffed. "I needed *my* own thing." She pointed to her chest.

"We were going to combine resources."

"This is a big city. Room enough for both of us. For the moment, I'm concentrating on fashion designers and that industry."

"You've already done this?" Charisse rubbed her forehead.

"A month ago. I have a small staff that's the face of the company. However, next week I will have a coming-out party of sorts. I'd like for you to come."

Charisse stood. She had to move, get her body engaged in an activity. One foot in front of the other was her motto. Keep moving forward. She headed to her office door and opened it wide. She ignored Shelby's call to her. Down the hall, past the framed photos, she moved as if someone had power over her body. Tracy looked up in confusion.

Not until she stood in front of Shelby's office did she realize why she was there.

"Charisse, you're scaring me." Shelby's voice took on a shrill note.

"What's going on?" Tracy whispered, as she swooped in on Charisse.

Shelby's name was on a plaque on the wall near the door. The care that had gone into picking the right frame and the right font didn't matter anymore. Charisse would have to get her mind wrapped around being the sole owner of New Vision.

Doubt did its dance in her gut. Waves of nausea swirled, ready to take her down the moment she showed any sign of weakness. She closed her eyes and took deep breaths.

When her nerves were slightly calmer, she opened her eyes. Her gaze focused on the nameplate. She removed Shelby's name and handed it to her.

"Goodbye, Shelby."

"Charisse, you're being childish. Let's talk about this."

Tracy stayed at her side. Her rigid stance resembled a soldier ready to protect, ready to deliver a powerful blow. Despite a slight stature, she more than made up for her physical limitations with a fierce glare.

"Jo." Charisse stood next to the receptionist's desk. "Could you take Shelby's name off the telephone listing?" She was amazed at the calmness of her voice.

"What's next? Are you going to kick me out?" Shelby's head bobbed at each word.

"You know, that's an excellent idea."

"Please, allow me the satisfaction." Tracy stepped between them.

"Don't you dare touch me." Shelby held her purse up as a shield.

Charisse touched Tracy's arm in case she'd have to restrain her overprotective assistant. Tracy didn't move an inch. Instead, her eyes shot laser beams of venom at Shelby, who was backtracking her way to the elevator.

Charisse turned, not bothering to wait for the elevator to arrive. Shelby's eviction was all that mattered.

"Is everything okay with you, Charisse?" Jo asked.

"Yes. It will be."

She walked back to her office and flopped onto the couch. Her phone rang, but she ignored it. As she stared up at the skylight, she had to admit that not even the clouds drifting past could raise the curtain of funk she was in.

"I'm not surprised," Tracy said, closing the door.

"Deep down inside, I knew she wasn't coming on board."

"Did she get a promotion?"

Charisse shook her head. "Opening a firm. *Has* opened a firm." She looked over at Tracy. "We're invited to the open house."

Tracy muttered a curse.

"I'm going to need a moment to get used to the new arrangement." Charisse kept her eyes closed.

"Do you want me to cancel Brent?"

"No." Charisse sighed. "I should be fine by this evening. I'll need to work on something to take my mind off…" *This betrayal.*

Tracy left, allowing her some much needed space. All her calls were routed to other employees. No one had to know the turmoil beneath the surface at New Vision.

By late afternoon, numbness had set into Charisse's spirit. Work still had to be done. Phone calls had to be made. Now she might have to hire one or two more employees to fill in the gaps in her staff. Tracy and Jo had popped into her office to let her know they were leaving. She didn't ask Tracy about her interview the next day. The timing couldn't be worse. She needed more clients to make the job secure enough for Tracy. Yet she couldn't take on more clients without someone like Tracy to assist her.

Her cell phone rang. It was Brent. She answered.

"I'm outside the office. The door is locked."

She hung up and hurried to the door.

He stood near the elevator bank, wearing a toothy grin and holding up a bag that looked like carryout food.

"Whatever you have smells good." Charisse hadn't realized that she'd skipped breakfast and lunch until the rich, savory aroma of the food permeated the office.

"Figured that I'm keeping you from dinner. Sorry."

"Guess we should get underway, then. What time is your flight?"

"I have a plane at my disposal. Whenever we're done, I'll take off for Boston. I'm hoping that we can map out a basic outline."

Charisse nodded. "Anyone ever called you a micromanager?"

"Not to my face. Are you going to?"

"I'll wait until you leave." She headed toward her office to get her files.

When she reemerged, she heard him in the kitchenette. The delicious smell pulled her in to the source.

"This is very thoughtful."

"I do manage sometimes. It's also my apology for being such a pain yesterday and possibly in the future."

"In that case, I may have to give you the menus for all my favorite takeout places." She surveyed the various boxes lining the table.

"Too much?"

"Nope." Charisse popped a box open and saw the fried rice. Her mouth watered. The next box contained Hunan chicken. The man had a knack for picking her favorites. She spotted the familiar name of the Chinese restaurant a block from the office. He must have pestered Tracy to learn all her favorites.

With the day she'd had, she'd take whatever peace offering she could have. Her rumbling stomach concurred.

"Don't be shy. Or else I'm going first." Brent held his paper plate in front of him.

"I do have a sharp weapon," she joked, holding up a fork.

They jostled with each other, jockeying for the prime position in front of each box of food. Soon Charisse had filled her plate with a sample of each dish. Brent followed her path around the table. Conversation remained light and neutral.

Charisse motioned with her head. "Let's go into the conference room."

She set down her food on the circular table. She took her seat and smiled when Brent took the seat next to her.

Brent looked up from his plate. "I'm working on getting the guys down here when I return at the end of the week."

"Good. I'd like to meet them and get to know them." She twirled lo mein around her fork. "Are we starting from scratch with them?"

"For the most part, yes. They have a website that's pretty crappy—kind of amateurish. One of the guys started a mailing list, but then that fell to the wayside. Now I think they're on the latest social networks."

"At least they're aware of all the small things that make a difference in today's scene. Would you pull up a few of the accounts so I can take a look?"

Brent had already pulled out his laptop. With a few keystrokes, he had their Twitter account on his screen. "Some of the stuff is pretty raw."

Charisse pushed away her half-eaten food and scooted closer to Brent. She read the shorthand note and almost choked.

"Click on his profile name, please." She read all the latest updates, which were in the same cryptic style. What the young man had managed to write made her shake her head in frustration.

"Keep going, please. Next one."

"I told you they were raw. I tried to explain to them about image and brand. They think that they're keeping it real." Brent brought up the next site.

Charisse grabbed a notepad. Time to write the list of dos and don'ts that needed immediate attention. Over the next hour, she had Brent bring up all their online sites.

"That was quite…ah…interesting." She rubbed her tired eyes.

"An understatement. They also have videos." Brent got up and stretched. He cleared the table of their forgotten plates.

Charisse looked at her watch but knew that she had to push through watching the videos to know what else was out there. This was a job that she'd normally give to Tracy. But, Brent had been adamant that only she work on the project, and with his hovering, she would have to review the online videos.

"While you watch the videos, I'll take care of all this food." Brent reclosed the boxes.

"You can put the food in the refrigerator. Someone always eats the leftovers."

Brent finished putting away the food. He debated with himself whether to show Charisse the underbelly of the group. The group's egos were proving to be their weak point. But hiding the messy details from her wouldn't help with finding the right road map for them. He hoped the journey wouldn't be too painstaking.

"Too much for you?" he asked when he returned to the room.

"It's a bit random, which makes branding difficult. The rawness is okay if that's the collective image of the band. I suspect it isn't, though. Let's get that nailed down before we allow the individual personalities to take over. Although by the look of how many friends and followers they have, it might be too late to contain the more colorful members of the group."

"The one thing I don't want is to sugarcoat who they are. All For One are four guys from different backgrounds, and despite their rough beginnings, they've formed a bond like brothers." Brent felt compelled to defend them when he saw the frown etched along her forehead.

"You know, whenever you talk about them, your voice softens." She played with a fortune cookie in her hand. "Tell me about your connection with them."

Charisse's voice coaxed him to share. This woman had a special knack for getting him to open up.

"I first saw them at a high school talent show." Brent paused. "At the time, I wasn't in the business as an agent. The instant that they took the stage the crowd went crazy. Their style reminded me of the R & B bands from the 1990s. They could sing, dance and knew how to work the audience. The icing on the cake was their passion." Brent broke off, a bit embarrassed at how much he had gushed. He looked at Charisse for her reaction. She remained quiet and thoughtful. At least her frown had been erased.

"I know what you mean. When I reviewed the concert footage you sent me, I have to admit that not only was I impressed but I immediately saw many viable possibilities. That made me excited." She smiled at him widely, and his body reacted as if jolted.

"Having the right person to do this project is paramount. But having someone like you, who is excited about the guys and their potential, is even more important."

"Thank you," she said with a quiet simplicity.

Brent didn't understand what was happening to him. He suddenly had the strong urge to rub his finger along her cheek until it rested on her soft lips. He didn't want to face the reality that only a separation could diminish his feelings.

He'd never pushed himself on a woman. Work usually served to kill any romantic efforts. Charisse, he suspected, was too much of a professional to be feeling the sparks he was feeling. He tried to refocus his mind.

Brent took a deep breath and plunged forward. "They also sang at my wife's funeral. She died in a car accident two years ago. In a way, I guess they do have more of a special connection with me than any other group."

"I'm sorry to hear about your loss." She covered his hand with hers briefly. The moment she removed her hand, he wanted to protest.

No one had sparked any iota of interest in him since his wife's passing. He'd grieved for Marjorie almost to the detriment of his health. Counseling and his career switch had helped him focus on the present and future. But he struggled to allow his guilt to dissipate.

"Tell me about the guys on that day," she asked softly.

"By the time they were done, there wasn't a dry eye. They sang a hymn a cappella with an abundance of soul that you're used to hearing from someone like Smokey Robinson, not this young group of guys. I definitely would love to issue it as a single. Of course their online presence doesn't quite go with a spiritual song."

"You're right. But there might be a way to spin this. More important, I can't wait to meet them."

Brent appreciated that Charisse had not barged ahead with tons of questions. Only recently had he been able to talk about his wife and begin reconnecting with friends. Each time, he tested his ability to be level-headed and normal again.

"I know that I can give them the platform they need to shine. Each one is gifted and can probably go solo, but in the meantime, we are focusing on them as a group."

Charisse nodded. "They've been performing long enough that I'm sure others have seen that special something that makes them memorable. Do you sing?"

Brent laughed. "Sorry, I'm sure it's a fair question. If you heard me, you'd probably change that to 'I hope you don't sing.'"

"I'm sure you have some talent. You know the business side, but I think there is also a love for music and performing in you."

"I can play the piano." Brent felt himself relax under her soft smile. "Used to play in a little jazz club during college."

"Oh, now I really want to see you play. I pictured you as the athletic type."

"Did all that, too. That's how I got scholarship money. But I wasn't a star, nor did I want to be one. Now I use my music to relax, to have fun."

"I'm betting that you can sing."

"Maybe one day you'll find out."

"One day…" Charisse grinned. Then her mood shifted. "Well, it's getting late. I think that I've got enough here to get started."

"Yes." Brent struggled to kill the intimate mood that had crept in quietly and settled softly around them.

The small windowless room stirred a longing in him. He didn't want to analyze it. How could he explain what he wanted most at that moment? *Don't even go there.* His brain, ever so logical, jabbed at his conscience. All he had to do was pull away and board his flight.

"Here's to hard work and success. Let's seal with a handshake." Charisse offered her hand.

Brent took her hand and nodded. "See you in two weeks."

He wanted to turn her hand over and softly place a kiss on her pulse. Would her heartbeat spike the way his did right now at the mere thought of the temptation?

Thankfully, he didn't have to think about the option. Charisse led the way out of the room. She chatted about always being there when the cleaning crew came through. He offered the expected nods and interested tilt of the head as he listened.

But he couldn't focus. Her new haircut allowed the tip of a rose tattoo to peep above the collar of her blouse.

"You were saying?" Charisse stopped and turned.

Brent almost bumped into her back. "Oh, I was… complimenting your new hairdo. Suits you." His hand rose to touch her hair.

Her face turned into his hand, perfectly molding into his palm. Before he could pull away his hand, she covered it with hers. Her gaze rested on his face, almost at his chin, before she scanned his face slowly, finally locking eyes with him.

He only hesitated for a second before lowering his mouth to seal his kiss.

Chapter 6

Brent accepted the sweet invitation of Charisse's parted lips. He couldn't believe that he was kissing her, and he cocooned her within his arms to savor the reality. Excitement zipped along his nerve endings like a caffeinated blast.

She moaned and settled against his taut body. He felt her curves, from the firm breasts, to her flat abs, to the small hips where his hands lightly rested. He didn't want to rush this, nor end it.

Yet he pulled back, a whispered breath apart.

"What…are you doing?"

"This is so wrong," Brent whispered.

"But it feels so right." She stood on tiptoe, sliding her body along his, flicking the On switch to his body. This time she had her hands locked firmly on his hips.

Brent groaned. He shook away the frail vapors of rules and decorum.

Desires flamed.

His mouth sought refuge at the spot under her ear-lobe. The perfume she must have dabbed there acted like an accelerant. He tasted her skin, seeking to know every part of her. His kisses peppered her face softly.

She unbuttoned his shirt. Her eyes were bright and filled with desire. He lifted her and placed her on the edge of the conference table. Her tongue seared a path down his chest.

He couldn't be outdone. His fingers clumsily worked to unbutton her shirt. His throat went dry.

The black lacy bra offered her breasts in a delectable display. She took his hand and allowed him to cup her breast. His thumb swept back and forth, teasing her aroused nipple.

"Allow me," she whispered. Her mouth looked tender and delicious, moist for the taking.

"Darn it, who cares," he muttered. He took it, claiming her mouth with a guttural charge.

Her hand reciprocated the attention by cupping him between his legs.

Their bodies touched, skin meeting skin. Their mouths celebrated their connection. He tasted her, enticed by her bold strokes. He craved hearing her moan against his lips. The sheer rapture of the moment reached addictive levels.

A phone rang.

The noise only barely penetrated the heightened sensuality of the moment. Finally, the ringing stopped.

Brent kissed Charisse's shoulder. Although she was beautiful in the lacy bra, he'd much rather it be off. Right now, he wanted to slowly suck her nipple. The thought almost made him explode.

The phone rang again.

"I think it's mine." Charisse released him and reached for the phone.

The minute she answered, he noticed a wave of realization cascade over her. He stepped back before she pushed him away. There was no mistaking the regret in her face. She grabbed her shirt and scooted off the table and out of the conference room.

Charisse had done some stupid things in her life. But this had to rank up there in the top three. Acting like a horny teen was one thing, if she was a teen. Now she had to face Brent and hope that he'd still want to work with her.

Never mind that he'd seemed turned on. Most men would take anything being offered—on the conference table, of all places. She wanted to cry but couldn't.

Deep down inside, she knew why she couldn't shed a tear. The remorse had left the building. She shook her head. In how many office gossip stories had she delivered her scathing opinion of office relationships and inappropriate client behavior?

Thankfully, Tracy had called to check up on her.

She only wished that she'd sounded a little less like she'd just woken. But she couldn't switch off the sexual energy that had her mind in a fog.

Now she wanted to go home. Her front door needed to be closed on Brent and his all-powerful sexiness. She needed to be gone in case Tracy took the initiative to come to the office to reassure herself that everything was okay.

Charisse tucked in her shirt, straightened her skirt and fiddled with her hair, which had decided not to cooperate. She took deep breaths before leaving her office. Right now, her emotions needed a sanctuary.

She almost jumped out of her skin when she opened the door and Brent stood there, as if he'd been waiting for her to reemerge.

"I am truly sorry," Brent blurted.

She nodded. "I should be the one apologizing. I shouldn't have…it's been a long day."

"I apologize for that, too. Sometimes I suffer from insomnia and think that the entire world does, too." Brent rubbed his forehead furiously. He walked away but then came back to stand in front of her.

"Yes?" Charisse braced herself for the tongue lashing that she expected from him.

"I am sorry. I meant no disrespect to you. Not trying to take advantage." His mouth pursed. Something troubled him, hanging over his shoulder like a weight.

"I'm fine," she said, hoping to ease him from his torture.

"It's just that I have no regrets. I liked kissing you. I enjoyed having you in my arms. I'm only sorry that I skipped so many steps without your consent." Although he looked pained with the admission, he never once avoided eye contact.

She was impressed. He could've brushed aside her feelings, headed out the door and pretended it didn't happen or, worse, thought that he had an open door to express his desires. Instead, he had stepped up like a man.

"Well, that's all I wanted to say."

"Hold on a second. You're not the only one who has the floor." She saw his shoulders square, and he took a deep breath. A small tic worked at his clenched jaw.

She wanted to lay a comforting touch on his jaw until he relaxed. But no, that had gotten her into trouble only minutes ago.

"I am ashamed for not showing proper restraint—and with a client, nonetheless. What happened tonight wouldn't or couldn't have happened with just anyone. I'd hoped that you'd kiss me. I'm glad that you did." The last statement almost caught in her throat. She tried to keep her gaze locked on those gray-blue eyes, but she suddenly felt shy. She lowered her gaze to her fingers that were nervously chipping away at her nail polish.

He grinned. "Whew, I'm so relieved."

"Me, too," she said, with her own wide grin.

"Now what?"

"We can't do this again," she said without conviction.

"You're right. We can't."

Charisse already knew that she'd be in trouble again. The only thing missing now was an opportunity. She'd find a way back into Brent's arms. Very little caused any sort of addictive behavior within her. Brent's influence had a searing effect on her nervous system and, try as she might, she couldn't make herself immune to it.

The memory of his hand stroking her breast made her catch her breath.

"Are you okay?" Brent hovered.

"Just a bit tired."

"I won't keep you any longer. It's time for me to get on that plane, anyway."

"Great. I'll walk out with you. Meet you back here in a few minutes? I'll gather my stuff. Believe it or not, I'll probably put in another hour of work when I get home."

"No one at home waiting for you?"

"No, I'm all alone." Charisse hadn't invited a man to her house in a long time. All she knew how to do was to add a tone of invite to her words. For her, being flirty was like cranking up a rusty, neglected tractor but that wouldn't stop her from trying.

Brent surveyed the area in the conference room. He made sure no evidence lingered of what had almost transpired. The only thing left to do was for the cleaning crew to come through, to vacuum and dust. Brent picked up his briefcase and turned out the light.

Time for him to return to reality.

But at least he'd have this night to remember. He appreciated that Charisse had not put him through the wringer. He wanted to believe that she did want him as much as he wanted her.

His doubts were underscored by the fact that they had only known each other for less than a week. But their instant attraction was undeniable. Yet that was only the beginning of what he felt. His attraction gave way to open respect and a desire to be with her. He wanted a friendship, too. But he refused to push himself on her and didn't know how far he could go.

He headed toward Charisse's office. He wondered why his phone hadn't rung all night. A check of the instrument revealed that he'd mistakenly turned it off. Hopefully there were no emergencies. He'd been too distracted to be aware of the rare uninterrupted evening.

His phone buzzed in the various messages and texts that now came through the system. One reminder was to get him headed to the airport. Realizing the time, he summoned his driver.

"Ready?" he asked.

Charisse walked toward him with bags in her hands. They headed to the elevator, taking the ride down together. No conversation, not even small talk, was shared between them. His thoughts centered on what she might be thinking at that moment. Did she regret sharing her desires?

When he pushed open the door, the brisk cool temperature hit them in the face. He wrapped an arm around Charisse to shield her from the wind.

As soon as the car stopped, he opened the door and helped her in. He waved to the driver to get back in the car.

"The weather turned a little brutal." He stated the obvious. "I didn't mean to shove you in the car."

"I appreciate the warmth. Seems like this spring weather is going to stay put for a little bit." She rubbed her legs, a move that tantalized him.

"Can I give you a lift somewhere?"

"I usually take the subway just a couple of blocks away."

Another gust of wind slammed litter against the car window. A trash can crashed onto its side and rolled back and forth as the breeze toyed with it.

"Like you said, it's much warmer in here. I'd be happy to drop you off at home."

"You have your flight. I don't want to put you out of your way."

"That's the beauty of chartering the plane. Besides, I'd feel better making sure you got home safely."

"You're going to spoil me with all these rides. I won't

know how to handle the subway with the masses. But you don't hear me protesting too much. And this forecast sure isn't working with my clothing choices."

"Where to?" Brent couldn't complain about the clothing choices. From his vantage point, her fashion sense was excellent. Her lingerie also had the power to invoke a massive coronary in him.

"I'm in Brooklyn, Brownsville neighborhood."

"The driver has a GPS. Go ahead and tell him your address."

Charisse shared the address with the driver, who punched in the information. Before long, they were heading through the busy streets, darting between the other vehicles and the pedestrians heading to the local bars.

Brent couldn't remember the last time that he hung out with friends after work. Even his employees usually left him at the office. What was there to celebrate? Work kept any dark, brooding thoughts out of his head. He'd never felt dissatisfied.

Somehow, in Charisse's company, he felt as if warm sunshine continually beamed down on him. Watching the evening crowd walking in their huddles, enjoying each other's company, did make him realize what he'd missed, or rather what he'd avoided.

"You like New York?" He turned from the window toward Charisse.

"All my life I've lived in New York—first upstate and now here. It's home. I'm glad that my plans came to fruition right in my backyard. There's no place like it, you know."

The evening lights refracted off the angle of her face, enhancing her fine bone structure with rich blue, crisp white and bloodred neon hues. Her eyes radiated an appreciation of the sights. He could tell the city had a firm hold on her heart.

"I know what you mean. Boston has its own big city vibe. It's constantly on the go."

"Yeah. It can be a bit busy." She shrugged. "I like the energy. It's like a shot of adrenaline."

"Yep, but I do like escaping and getting back to Boston."

"Boston isn't a slouch, either. Pretty fast-paced, too."

He chuckled. "You've got to come my way and check out the city."

"Maybe."

He didn't push it. It wasn't as if he could pretend that he had a meeting or any other business-related reason to get her there.

She looked past him through his window. "Looks like I'm in the old familiar neighborhood."

Brent turned to take it all in. He wondered if her neighborhood was a good match to her personality. From outside, the brownstone homes with white trimmings were the same. Only a visit on the inside could tell him more. But after what he'd done earlier, he could forget ever getting an invite to her home.

"Brent, thank you for getting me home safely and in comfort. This has been quite the week."

"I hope in a good way."

"Definitely." She scooted out of the car when the driver held open the door. "See you in a couple of weeks?"

Brent nodded.

Fourteen days before he would see her again. Hearing only her voice on their business calls would be torture.

"Good night," she said. A smile tried to emerge but was swallowed by the indecision that crossed her face. "Have a safe flight."

Brent couldn't stay in the car. Impulsively, he got out to escort her to her door.

"You don't have to walk me to the door."

"True." He didn't turn around but continued up the short path to the front door.

There, Charisse turned to him. His thoughts were incoherent, and everything he wanted to convey stayed in. Maybe it should.

She leaned into him and kissed his cheek.

He squeezed his eyes shut and clenched his jaw, trying to remain a gentleman. If only she knew how she'd further branded him with her soft lips.

Then she unlocked her door and stepped in. She leaned her head against the door, waiting.

Brent didn't want to ask to be invited in. If only he could be so cavalier. He'd never been that sort of man. No way that he'd start now, despite his body's awakening to this woman's touch.

All it would take was for him to wave off his driver and forget the meetings he had in Boston. He could cross the doorway with one foot in front of the other and close the door, shutting out any intrusive thoughts. And then he could let the remainder of the night unfold, without rules getting in the way.

Instead, he rubbed his cheek with the back of his hand. Time to go.

He did have the driver wait as Charisse turned on

the lights in the house. Satisfied that she was fine, he settled back for the ride to the airport. Alone.

He considered texting her something short and sweet. But what to say? *Why can't I get our kiss out of my mind?*

Brent grinned.

He left his phone in his pocket. Instead, he savored the memories until he could be back in New York City.

Chapter 7

Boston was home and all that was familiar and dependable to Brent. Yet he felt restless and a bit cranky. Sleep had eluded him by the time he'd got in from New York. His entire weekend had dragged, even as he caught up with his work. By eight o'clock on Monday morning, he refused to stay in bed any longer.

Instead of heading straight to the office, he went to the gym. Maybe working out the nameless cause of his frustration would put him on an even keel. Brent threw his gym bag into the bottom of his locker and hung up his suit. Time to get his muscles bulked up and toned and this restless energy evaporated.

Rochester, one of his buddies from college, doubled as his personal trainer. However, the sight of his impeccably fit friend waiting, with a too-wide grin, made him want to rethink the start of his day. The nickname Rocky suited his rock-hard physique. The man looked as if he'd eaten a thousand protein bars for breakfast. Brent slowed his approach as he wondered what body part was about to be taxed to the point of failure.

"Where have you been for the past few days?" Rocky greeted Brent with a mock jab to his pec.

"In the Big Apple. I'll probably be going there a bit more over the next few weeks." Brent glanced at the usual crowd of workout enthusiasts already pumping weights, jogging like their lives depended on it on the treadmills or pumping their legs on the elliptical machines.

"Sounds like the business is kicking. Knew you'd have another success in your pocket."

"I'm not celebrating hard."

"We'll see, 'cause it looks like you've been packing away those carbs in the city. You can celebrate yourself right onto this, champ." Rocky rested his hand on the elliptical machine. His grin showed off his shiny white veneers.

His short journey on the professional bodybuilding circuit had earned him enough fame and money to open the fitness center.

"You've got to make up for missing valuable workout days. I can already tell that you didn't hit any gyms. I've known you long enough to know that you'd work yourself to exhaustion."

Brent pushed against the machine's resistance. Working out had never been about vanity. His body didn't add weight the way his friends complained about their situations. As part of getting his life back in sync, his counselor had suggested a routine of healthy, physical labor. Rocky took up the charge to help. His friend also had a sensitive side that talked about reconnecting with family and friends.

"I'm impressed. You're not winded. New York must have agreed with you."

"Understatement." Brent breathed heavily as the program kicked into hill mode. His thighs were on the verge of exploding.

"More traveling involved?"

Brent nodded. Sweat trickled down his face—only five more minutes before his warm up ended.

"Did I tell you that I have a niece who sings?"

Brent shook his head. He knew what was coming next.

"I have her CD in the car. She thinks that this is what she wants to do. Her parents, especially my brother, are dead against it because they don't want her wasting her time." Rocky tossed Brent a towel. "I'm only the uncle, but this girl is good in school. She's in a bunch of after-school stuff. And she can sing her heart out. This isn't about her trying to skip her education or anything like what my brother and his wife think."

"Call my secretary. Get your niece on my schedule. No promises, though."

Many friends and even strangers approached him with the hope that he would open the door for them. He'd learned at the beginning not to automatically say no, in case there was indeed a gem of talent. But he'd also learned to tell the truth if he couldn't or wouldn't help them. It didn't always go over well, but he refused to take advantage of people's dreams.

"What happened in New York City? Any celebrity gossip? Any leading ladies need a good-looking male escort?"

Brent shook his head. Speaking proved to be difficult. His thighs burned and felt like rubber. His lungs could only give him enough air to breathe—nothing else. He counted down the ten second cooldown before he could limp off the machine.

Rocky clapped his massive hands. "Now you're all warmed up. Let's head to the weights. Upper body, today."

"Would you leave me alone if I told you that I met a woman?" Brent asked.

"Whoa!"

Brent rested his hands on his knees, hunched over to buy more rest time, as Rocky tried to recover from his shock. Rocky had promised to turn him into a babe-magnet, but frankly he didn't want a bunch of women harassing him. Now his friend considered his project a major success.

"Fill in the details."

Brent filled in the basics about Charisse and their meeting.

"You went from no prospects to mixing business with pleasure."

"There's no mixture. I don't plan to stir up anything. My attention and commitment need to stay focused."

Rocky's only response was to hand him heavy weights.

Within the hour, Brent had warmed up, pumped and burned his muscles and was now stretching away the aches as much as possible.

"Okay, enough. You're trying to kill me."

"It's better than knocking sense into you. I wish I could have a few words with Charisse."

Brent grinned. "Instead of messing with my personal

life, I have another project to keep you busy. Interested in working out four young guys who may be more talk than action? The time frame is now, for two weeks." Maybe the same advice that worked on him could work on the guys.

"Sure. Every client counts."

"Great. These guys are coming to the group with both good and bad habits. They have to learn to be a team and put all the petty B.S. aside. One way to learn discipline is through hard work. You get my drift."

"You pick the day that we can start rocking and rolling." Rocky cracked his neck. The evil grin appeared.

"I'll give you a call later today with the details."

He fist bumped Rocky before heading to the shower.

Brent entered the main office, still trying to adjust his tie. He'd squeezed an hour and a half into his schedule for the gym. The workout had helped to erase his crankiness. From the sound of the phones ringing and his hustling staff, he would have to hit the ground running.

"You're late, Brent," Vicki, his personal assistant, said.

"Just by a few minutes."

She wasn't amused.

"Actually, it's more like thirty minutes. You obviously forgot your appointment with the Powerhouse label when you headed off to play at the gym."

"Oh. I remember now." Brent stepped into a nearby cubicle. "Is he mad?" He craned his neck to see down the hall into his own office.

"He's in there drinking tons of coffee."

"Thanks, Vicki."

"For heaven's sake, your tie is a mess." She grabbed his tie. "You don't usually forget meetings. What's going on?"

Brent tried to walk away when she was done, but her death grip hadn't loosened. "Now you're making me late."

When Vicki had her mind to it, he couldn't make her budge. His choice for an assistant was someone who had the maturity and wisdom to think ahead of him, keep him on track and work above and beyond expectations. Vicki came with all of those abilities and a few that emerged in times of need. She had her 1950s-style hairdo and impeccable dress sense in skirt suits, black pumps and her glasses, which always slid to the end of her nose. He'd offered her shares in the business because she was worthy of a partnership.

"Go. Work your magic. Then I'll be in there for a debriefing."

He saluted her and headed for his office. The long hallway felt like the walk of shame. His staff stopped their tasks to watch him go into the office. He promptly adjusted the blinds to keep out prying eyes.

"Mr. Caldwell, I wasn't expecting you." Right label, but wrong person. "I thought I'd be meeting with Glenn Holder." Should he be worried that his meeting with the executive manager of the Powerhouse record label had been switched to the CEO?

"I took the appointment. Pulled rank," said Caldwell with a certain arrogance. "And Francine wanted me to intercede on her behalf."

Brent almost coughed. More than the back of his throat itched. His body instantly chilled.

"We'll get to Francine soon enough." Caldwell

pointed a thick finger at him. "Although you kept me waiting, I won't hold it against you. Haven't been to Boston in a while."

"I'm listening."

"First quarter numbers coming in. The downward trend doesn't look good. Some acts will be cut. So far I've managed to keep yours off the list."

Brent didn't like what he was hearing one bit. Powerhouse was known as a small but successful, label that focused on building young artists. He had three artists already signed to the label, including All For One.

While Caldwell had delivered his news with a certain level of enjoyment, Brent had focused on keeping calm. What was being said aloud was only part of the message. Caldwell had taken on the role of messenger for another reason.

"The single by All For One has to be released by the beginning of summer to take advantage of kids being out of school. We need tours, appearances. You need buzz."

"Are they in jeopardy of being dropped?"

"No. But the business can have a cruel edge to any performer's career." Caldwell leaned forward. His face was inviting, but his eyes remained cold. "We go way back, so I won't B.S. you. If they were on the list, convince me that these guys deserve an extension."

Brent hated the brutality of the entertainment industry—not that the legal arena didn't have its own savage approach to success. He'd learned to navigate those shark-infested waters, too. This was new territory, but he wasn't about to sweat under Caldwell's scrutiny.

"I've got a public relations firm that will zero in on what they need. I'm working on their image. You can trust that the guys will have the necessary media blitz leading up to the debut."

"We'll want them to come to the office and record an acoustic version for the label's website. That's a tradition."

Now that tone was more like it, Brent thought. "Sounds fantastic. I'll get the date for that," he replied.

Brent wasn't about to sigh with relief. However, Caldwell mentioning something as long-term as recording and posting an acoustic performance boded well.

"Now, on the matter of Francine… My daughter is enamored with you. I don't normally get involved with her love life. But this is the first time that she's asked for my help." Caldwell laughed. "I feel like a matchmaker."

Brent couldn't nod or shake his head. Even his breathing seemed to be waiting on the bombshell.

"I'm inviting you to my house in the Hamptons with my family and a few friends. It's my wife's birthday."

"I'd be honored, but I feel a bit awkward attending your wife's birthday. We haven't ever met."

Caldwell shrugged. "You're not coming because of my wife. You're coming because of Francine."

"Again, thank you, but I can't."

"Really?"

Brent didn't consider diplomacy to be one of his strengths. How strongly could he protest without losing too much? "I'll try my best." His tone was flat, devoid of any sincerity.

"Good. Now my little girl can stop being a pain about this matter." Caldwell stood and adjusted his suit.

"When is the party?" Brent kept his fingers crossed.

"In two weeks. You do this for me, and I'll be sure to put the guys on the lineup for the Times Square event."

Brent held back further protest. There had to be a way out of this mess but still get what he wanted for the group. But Caldwell's standing with his chest puffed out in the middle of his office wasn't helping him to concentrate on any plan.

They wrapped up the meeting with a minor discussion about the band and Brent's switch in careers. Finally Vicki, who always managed to intrude on his meetings if they went too long, came to his office door. He allowed her to escort Caldwell out of the office.

He was looking out of the window when Vicki returned to his office and closed the door.

"From Caldwell's happy ramblings, I'd say that the meeting was successful. From your demeanor, I think the jury is still deliberating."

"Something like that." Brent didn't want to present his assistant with his predicament. Too much information would have to be revealed about Charisse. One thing he did know for sure—Francine was going to be a wedge in his business affairs and personal life.

"What do you want me to work on?" Vicki had her pen and pad ready for his directions. Whatever conclusion she may have arrived at stayed hidden behind her business facade.

"Were you able to get All For One on a flight to New York?"

"Yes. They'll fly out two weeks from now on Thursday evening. You didn't say how long you wanted them out there. I have the time tentatively set for through the weekend."

"That'll work for now. We'll probably have to relocate them for a short bit to New York."

"I'll check into that. In the meantime, they're booked in some small venues here to capitalize on the hometown appeal before heading to New York." Vicki's pen moved across the page, filling the space with copious notes.

"Sounds good. I'll head to New York on Thursday. Keep me out there for a week. If it ends up being shorter, I'll let you know."

"I don't have anything scheduled in New York for you that week. Was I supposed to make calls?"

"No. I decided at the last minute to stay there. I just hired a new PR firm, and my schedule for now will be focused on pushing the new band."

Vicki looked over the top of her glasses at him. "You have a ton of acts knocking on your door. All their proposals are in your office. Do you want me to farm them out?"

"Let me take a look at them first, and then I'll pluck out the ones that I want to listen to. I can do that in New York." Brent sensed Vicki's hawkish skills homed in for clues on what was going on. He wanted to be alone. "Anything else?"

"Your mother called."

"And?"

Vicki flipped over pages on her pad and cleared her throat. "I was instructed to write this down."

"Don't bother reading it." He flicked his fingers for the note. His mother often went to extremes to make a point. If his mother felt neglected, she could pester him on a number of topics, like whether he was eating properly, did he finally hire a gardener or something as ridiculous as whether he would be attending his cousin's girlfriend's sister's best friend's baby shower. Or she would return with the earnest request for him to reconcile with his brother.

"If she asks, I'm going to tell her that you wouldn't allow me to read it. Not going to get yelled at by your mother." Vicki ripped off the page and placed it on the desk in front of him. "My job is done. I will talk to you later. I have real work to do."

Brent waited until Vicki left him before he looked down at the square yellow sheet. In Vicki's neat handwriting, he read his mother's request to tell her when would be a good time for her to visit.

"Visit?" he asked aloud.

He walked over to his desk and picked up the phone. Again he read the request. His head furrowed as he tried to remember if he'd made a promise to her that he now had forgotten.

Nothing came to mind, except her plea that he come visit more often. Once a season was good enough. Being held captive under her watchful attention was too much. After Marjorie's death, his mother hovered to the point of suffocating him.

Brent called his parent's house.

"Mom?" He could barely hear her over the noise in the background. The din behind her voice made conversation difficult.

"Brent, I can't talk now. I'm playing poker with some friends."

"It's the morning, Mom."

"Since when does poker require a certain time? We're having our tournament. Wish me luck."

"Good luck." He almost hung up before he remembered her cryptic message. "Is everything okay? I got your message."

"We'll talk later." Her voice dropped low.

Brent strained to hear. But he couldn't go any further with the conversation because the dial tone was the only sound in his ear.

What the heck was going on? Unease rippled through him.

He called his father.

"Brent? How's it going?"

"Fine. I wondered if you knew why Mom was calling me to visit." His parents had separated when he was a teen but still had a friendly on-again, off-again relationship that took the sting off an otherwise sordid episode of his life. Yet their still-married but separated status made for some quirky and memorable family dinners.

"Don't know. She hasn't said anything to me. What else is new with you?"

Brent chatted a little about his business. At least his father didn't badger him into visiting, although he was due a visit because they were supposed to go fishing.

"Maybe she called about your brother or sister."

"I saw Fontana a week or so ago, she's fine." Brent pursed his lips. "What about Harry?"

"All I heard is that he's moving to Boston."

The news had the same power as a punch to the gut.

Brent pursed his lips. "Harry's coming here? When?" His tone turned curt.

"Don't know all the specifics. Maybe he wants to make amends."

"Some things are best left alone." He didn't want to think about his brother. He certainly didn't want to deal with him in his home city.

"Don't expect your mother to leave things alone. She's determined to have you and your brother speaking by year's end."

Brent hated the drama of family conflicts. He'd done his best to walk away and not prolong any discord. However, his mother had taken up the cause. For an unknown reason, his brother was moving to Boston. Suddenly getting to New York seemed more urgent.

"You know, Brent, he is blood."

"Too bad he didn't remember that." Brent closed his eyes refusing to go down the path of hurt and anger.

His father sighed. "I'm heading off to the golf course. I'll chat with you later."

"Sure. Talk to you later." Brent hung up. His mood felt dark and heavy. He picked up the phone again. "Vicki, I'll head out to New York at the beginning of the week, instead of Thursday."

"Any other plans need to be rescheduled or made?"

"No. Something came up. The guys can still come up on Thursday." He hung up with Vicki.

His cell phone rang. He saw Charisse's name pop up on the screen. A welcome blast of fresh air for a funky morning.

"Charisse, good to hear from you."

"Hi, Brent. I have some good news."

"Go on."

"I got an interview with Gladys Beecher, the cable TV mogul."

"Hey, that's fantastic."

"One tiny thing. She wants the guys in her studio by Wednesday evening."

"Whoa! That's fast."

"I know. I know. Sorry. Another person fell through

for the spot. I called at the right time. She was interested with what I said about the group. Can you make it happen?"

Brent didn't know how he'd pull it off, but that's why he had Vicki. "Sure can. This is great. Just the shot in the system that they need."

"Good. I'll look forward to seeing you then." Her voice softened.

"Me, too." Brent suddenly sat up, realizing that he'd slipped down in the seat and had the phone cradled between his ear and shoulder. He couldn't help the silly grin.

"By the way, there's also a breakfast planning meeting on Thursday about the summer tour series."

"Isn't that too late for the guys to get on board?"

"I've got a friend who is one of the organizers. Should be able to get them in the lineup. It won't be the greatest spot, although they will be able to participate in the meet-and-greet session."

"I'm impressed. Friends in high places, huh? I'm looking forward to hearing more about it."

The Times Square event with the label's up-and-coming acts was a major accomplishment. And having the group placed on the summer tour was huge. His day had finally been turned around with good news. The bonus was that he'd see Charisse much sooner than anticipated.

"Well, I better get going. Or I'll be rambling on and keeping you from your work."

"I'm glad you called. I was thinking about you. I mean…I've been wondering what you had in mind for the group. But looks like you've managed to hit the ground running."

"I'm excited to work with All For One. I have a gut feeling that once the public sees and hears from them that they will attach to them in a major way. We'll blow up the internet with them."

"What about getting them into print magazines? I know that magazines are taking a hit with advertising revenue, but the younger kids still do like their posters."

"I've got some calls in. Problem is that there is no hype around them. That's why I'm hoping Gladys's coverage can give them a small boost to start something."

"They've got a decent back story that should connect with the girls. I've even arranged for them to meet with a personal trainer. Getting them ready for photo ops. Besides, I want them to work off some of the frustration that occurs in all group dynamics."

"That's smart thinking. Whether we like it or not, the visual package is as important as the talent."

"They're good-looking. With a toned physique and the right wardrobe, the posters and other print work will fall into place."

"True, true. I do have some connections with a few young designers. Young and hungry. They're also looking for that chance to be discovered. The right photo, in the right magazine, with mention of the designer is a coup."

"As long as it's F-R-E-E," Brent reminded.

Charisse laughed and Brent found himself joining in.

The sound of their laughter carried through the phone with a mysterious power that washed over him, making him relax and shake off his earlier brooding.

She could've called to talk about the weather, and he would feel the same. He wanted to be in her company.

Whatever door he had desperately kept shut now had been cracked wide enough for his emotions to flood through the opening. Part of him remained uneasy that not only did she have the power to shift his mood but she had the power to stir up emotions of pure joy that he hadn't felt in years. The momentum swept him off his feet in a way that left him feeling giddy but unsteady— a quite unfamiliar state.

"Can I get a repeat invite to that Cuban restaurant when I get there?" Brent wanted to relive the magical moment of when they'd first met.

"Ah, so you've become a convert of Luisa's cuisine? That was fast. I thought that I'd have to do some heavy convincing to get you to see my side of things. Are you always this impulsive?"

"Not really. Seems to be a new habit."

"I like it." Her voice sounded breathless. Sexy. Alluring.

"How about dinner with me sometime this week?" Brent grimaced over his eagerness. "Not that it's a date or anything."

"Right." She laughed. "No dating. I have my rules. But if I'm going to have dinner with you then how about a rain check for brunch with me?"

"As long as you know the boundaries," he teased.

"I'll be sure to reread my contract."

Brent laughed.

A knock on his office door interrupted him. Before he could erase the grin, Vicki popped her head into his office. She mouthed her message, eyebrows wiggling as if they delivered a separate message. She stuck out her wrist and tapped her watch.

"Hold one moment, Charisse." He pressed the mute button and then gave his full attention to his assistant.

"Your briefing with Vernon and Judith was five minutes ago." She stood in front of him looking like the school principal, glaring down at him.

"Thanks." He waited for her to leave before pressing the mute button. "Charisse, it looks like I have to head to a meeting. Thanks for the good news. I'm impressed."

"Glad to hear."

Brent ended the call regretfully. He'd been on a roll before Vicki had invaded his office. Since she wasn't bothering to retreat, he wasn't about to give her any ammunition to lecture him.

"What's got you looking like you're suffering from a gas attack, Vicki?"

"I barely heard from you when you went to New York. You've been distracted all day. The meeting with Caldwell seemed tense. And now you're missing a meeting and seem fine about it."

"Sounds like you're judging me." Brent stood up, on the defense.

"Sorry. I didn't mean to overstep."

Brent was used to Vicki's perfectionist ways and her attempts to make him fall into line. But listening to her highlight his recent faux pas raised his defenses. Especially when he knew he was guilty.

The fact that he was running around like a lovesick teenager at the detriment of his company pricked at his conscience. There was no doubt in his mind that Charisse was a special person. He just wasn't sure where she fit between his life and work.

Chapter 8

Charisse sipped her coffee, humming to the tune that played on the radio in her apartment. Today was a big day. She knew Tracy expected to hear about her status from the job interview. Another contract was due to be wrapped up with signing on a bakery. And Brent was due to arrive at her office to prepare for the interview with his group in two days.

Such an important day required the right outfit. Fashion wasn't her strong point, although she could pass muster. But she wanted to feel confident with everything coming at her today. With her coffee mug in hand, she stood in her closet studying the clothes. Her hand trailed over the various blouses. She hoped a color or style would jump out at her.

Did she want her neck to be visible? Should she wear an orange-red or chocolate-brown blouse or go with the blue one that always got her compliments? Pants or dress?

She blushed as she recalled the heavy flirting over the phone. What if Brent thought it was sexy? What if she did take the mild flirtation up one notch? What if she made that invitation to brunch follow a romantic evening?

The idea shocked her. Charisse took a gulp of coffee and almost had to spit the overly hot liquid.

She quickly showered and dressed, shoving aside any musings that were arousing more than her interest. Her reflection in the bathroom mirror over the sink allowed her to cast a critical eye on her clothing choice—peacock-blue blouse, black slacks and matching blazer. Now for a touch of makeup, and she was done.

"Darn it!" She set down the blush brush, turned out the lights and walked out the bathroom. Her makeup technique seemed rusty this morning.

Some independent career woman she was turning out to be. Planning her outfit for a man was such a wrong move. She wasn't the type of sophisticated socialite who traveled in Brent's circles.

When was the last time she'd dated? All the nuances of courtship were lost on her. Why would she bother to date with a six-to-one ratio of women to men in the city? But that would only matter if she had long-term expectations anyway. Keeping it casual would allow her the space to protect her feelings. She was determined to play the game like the men.

She knew just the person to call for help.

She grabbed her phone and started dialing.

"June, it's Charisse. How are things?"

"I'm heading to work. What's up, my friend?"

"Are you going out tonight?"

"Heading to the usual happy hour. You need me to do something for you?"

"Wondered if I could hang with you."

"Say what? You're going to leave your office and come to happy hour?" June chuckled. "I'm expecting an eclipse for that event."

June wouldn't be the only friend to freak out about her request. Social activities had been put on hold. Running the company got all her attention. As a result, her friends had drifted away.

Charisse cleared her throat. "Be quiet. It's about time I get out there."

"Really? Sounds like we may need to talk, instead of drink."

"Nope. Not ready to do any heavy-duty talking. Just need to be in a busy place." Charisse bit her lip, wondering if she should ask. "Do you believe in instant attraction?" Her heart pounded.

"Nope."

"Just like that? Why not?" Charisse would have answered just as definitively two weeks ago.

"'Cause that's in the movies. You know, when you finish seeing a film and you sigh and go away with that warm, gooey feeling. Doesn't happen in reality."

"Okay."

"Instant attraction is when it's only physical, nothing below the surface."

Charisse nodded. She didn't know how to argue the point without revealing her personal stake.

"I've got to run. Come by the office this evening, and we'll go out together."

"I'll be there," Charisse responded. Maybe this wasn't such a good idea.

"We'll see. You know I'm expecting you to cancel."

Charisse snorted. "Thanks for being supportive at a time when I need you."

"I'll stop giving you a hard time. Bye, sweetie."

Charisse hung up, her mood much improved. She'd forced herself to ignore Brent's charm. The man scrambled her ability to think straight. The giddy, silly feeling when she talked to him frankly embarrassed her. If they were going to work together, she had to pull herself in line. Otherwise, she'd be like those colleagues who everyone had fun gossiping about at happy hour.

Time to head to the office.

The morning temperature had warmed up over the weekend. Her blazer provided sufficient cover for the short walk to the subway. She opened her front door, and saw a man standing there, his hand poised to knock. She screamed in surprise, and her breath seized in her throat. Her heart beat wildly—partly from fright but also from delight as she recognized the person poised to knock on the door.

"Surprise!" Brent said.

"Wow!" Charisse exclaimed. "I can't believe you're here." She wanted to reach out and touch his face. Was he real? No mistaking those gray-blue eyes that always turned her on. Her breathing felt erratic. Remaining calm and cool would require all of her energy.

"I arrived early this morning. Wasn't sure if I would be on time."

"On time?"

"Yeah, for this."

Brent wrapped his arms around her in a close embrace. Charisse didn't have time to respond, because her body reacted instantly. She backed up into the house under his momentum. The door closed with a decisive slam.

"Brent," she gasped between his kisses. Her knees threatened to give way.

"Charisse." He sighed against her neck.

She tried speaking. Every time she opened her mouth, Brent covered it with his mouth. Stopping him never entered her thoughts. Why should she stop the pleasure that he was delivering to her body?

Well, if she couldn't use her words to respond, her body would do all the talking. She welcomed his embrace, while pressing her body against his muscled frame.

His mouth communicated its own language. Lips pressed against her throat, and the swirl of tongue blazed a trail that played at a special spot behind her ear. She squeezed her eyes shut, but it didn't stop the low moan of her arousal.

The clothes that she'd so diligently selected were now in the way. She wanted to feel his skin under her fingers, feel his toned physique and the ripple of his muscles as he moved. She pushed him away and unbuttoned her shirt.

"Down the hall." Charisse threw her blouse at his face. She unhooked her bra and dropped it at her feet.

No way would she feel shy under his steady gaze. She teased him by covering her breasts with her arm while coaxing him along the hallway to her bedroom with her other hand. She laughed at his agonized expression. Her heels tapped as she walked with an extra swing of her hips.

Before she made it to the doorway, Brent had grabbed her hips and pulled her back to him. He lifted away her hair from the back of her neck and kissed her rose tattoo, tracing the outline with his tongue. His hand made its acquaintance with her waist. His finger tickled her as it followed the path of her panties down to her inner thigh.

She sucked in air.

"You'd better exhale before you pass out," he whispered against her ear.

As if to coax her into obeying, his hand cupped her breast. He held her as if she belonged to him. No protest came from her. Total surrender was on her mind.

His warm touch over her nipple raised her pulse to a heated crescendo, matching the arousal between her legs. The man made her hot and needy for him. Right now she wanted more than an experimental foray. She ached for him to enter her and to satisfy her primal hunger for his sexual attention.

She barely remained still for him as he unzipped and pulled down her skirt.

"I like that look," he complimented.

She stood in her black pantyhose and three-inch pumps. He circled her. His fingers steadily worked the buttons of his shirt. His arousal stretched against his boxers. Her mouth went dry. The thought of riding him sent a shiver through her. His hand smoothed her behind and cupped it with a gentle squeeze.

"Is this for real?" she asked. She was afraid to close her eyes for too long, in case she awoke, frustrated and horny.

Brent knelt in front of her, looking up into her face. He tweaked her nipples. As her hips came closer to his face, her stomach brushed his cheek. His stubbled chin heightened the glorious sensation. She grabbed his head to remain upright.

"Nope. No hands." He looked up at her.

Now his hands rolled down her panty hose in slow motion while his fingers stroked her legs. He kissed the apex between her legs, then offered a flutter of kisses from her panty line down her inner thigh, where his finger had made its discovery. His tongue darted out and stroked her. She gave up because she couldn't help herself. Her hands continued to grab his head, but he gently restrained her, pushing her hands away.

She struggled to obey with barely any willpower intact.

Once out of the confines of the hose and pumps, Charisse walked over to her bed. She tossed back the cover and climbed in, leaving the cover flipped open for him to follow.

Instead, he stripped and donned a condom. She appreciated him being open with his desire to protect them both.

"Don't keep me waiting." She tapped the empty spot next to her.

"Impatient?"

"You have no idea." She propped herself on her arm to look down at him as he lay next to her.

She planted a hard kiss on his mouth. "Gosh, I love your lips."

This time when she lowered her head, he pulled her next to him and drove his tongue into her ready mouth. Their intimate language was more than chemistry—it transmitted desire and need. Each was sensitive to the other's probing and reactions.

He rolled her over, pinning her down. Her chest heaved from the foreplay, and her body was ready for his entry. She grasped him with her thighs, providing the invitation. He answered her call.

His movements came swift and deep, as she'd expected, as she'd hoped. Her body stayed in the moment, living every second in full, robust fashion. Her fingers gripped his backside, holding him in place, edging closer to the precipice.

"Let's do it." Brent groaned. His eyes squeezed shut. His teeth bared in a grimace.

Charisse couldn't utter any words. She obeyed. Holding on to each other, they took the leap, no safety net to stop them. Every ounce of her energy poured into the jump. In waves, they came together, over and over, until she was left empty and spent.

Charisse waited until her heartbeat stopped pounding in her head. "I'm thirsty." She got up and pulled on her dressing gown. "Water?"

Brent nodded. His face was buried among the pillows. "You must be a marathon runner."

Charisse giggled. Their light banter helped ease the doubts that slowly rose under the harsh light of reality. Yet Charisse toyed with the idea of establishing some type of rules of engagement—one way to make their relationship work. As she poured water into each glass, she was sure that she wanted an extension on their fun.

"You're thinking too hard." Brent took the glass. "Thanks."

"And you'd rather not?" She watched him gulp down his water.

"Don't think you'll give me much choice." He winked.

Charisse's shoulders relaxed. Maybe she didn't want to push hard for answers, anyway. Her life seemed to have taken a sharp detour, and she had a feeling there were a few blind curves in the immediate future.

They dressed and, for the second time, Charisse headed toward her front door on her way to work. This time Brent accompanied her after a lovemaking session that still left her breathless from the vivid recollection.

Brent's driver opened the passenger door and lightly touched his head. For Charisse, stepping into the car was like walking slowly toward further temptation. Everything about Brent had a lasting impact.

It didn't help that Brent sat back against the seat with a devilish smile. He'd taken a quick shower and donned his signature scent. The crisp, woodsy scent provided her with an aromatherapy session that made her want to close her eyes and roll naked in his shirt.

He was talking to her, but she could barely focus on his words. Her eyes lit on the shape of his mouth as it formed each word, then broke into a wide smile. She smiled back, thinking that he was the sexiest man alive.

"Are we going to have a standoff?" Brent asked.

Charisse shook her head, still frazzled. She scooted farther onto the seat next to him. He looked cool and amused.

"Regrets already? You make me feel like a predator." Brent sounded hurt.

Charisse slowly shook her head. "It's a bit soon for me to make sense of anything."

"I have no expectations."

Charisse nodded. She was the one who should be

telling him not to have any expectations. His casual attitude left her unsettled. He'd never know.

"Were you planning to come to the office before the interview with Gladys?" she asked.

"Yes. Unless it's going to be a problem?"

"No. No problem at all." Charisse was bone-weary tired. Her thoughts couldn't stick on anything but Brent. She had to remind herself that her feelings could get too intense for a business relationship. No matter how badly she wanted something to occur.

"I do have the vacant office for your use. No problem at all."

"Good. I was hoping that you'd keep the invite extended. I like working in your office. Good energy."

Brent had placed his arm along the seat behind her. Every action by this man drove her to distraction and weakened her resolve. She wished that she had it in her to relax and lean back against his arm. Without breaking her cool demeanor, she stayed at the corner of the seat and only talked about local news until they reached the office.

The minute Charisse walked through her office doors, she saw Jo's eyes widen. Her receptionist shifted her gaze back and forth between her and Brent.

"Good morning, Jo. Brent will be using the spare office today. By the way, is Tracy here yet?"

"Yes, she's here. Welcome, Brent."

Brent clearly had wound Jo around his finger. She'd never dropped her voice and smiled so sweetly for Charisse.

"Thanks for the warm welcome, Jo. Looks like I'll have the pleasure of your hospitality." He grinned and added a wink with his response.

Charisse tensed. The man was a born flirt. The red flags waved at full blast.

"Looks like you have new staff." Brent motioned with his chin.

"Yep." Charisse led him over to the intern who Jake had recommended. "This is Zoe from the grad program with NYU."

"Nice to meet you. You couldn't have picked a better place for your internship."

Charisse studied Brent's face to see if there were any signs that he was poking fun at her business. Instead, he looked sincere and was staring intently at Zoe, as if he were going to hypnotize her into feeling the same.

"And the young man sitting outside your office is Lance. He was on vacation last week." Charisse led him over to the cubicle.

"Hey, good to meet you." Brent shook hands with Lance.

"And your resident drill sergeant is at her desk."

This time Brent led the way to Tracy's desk. Charisse followed. His familiarity with her office pleased her.

"Hi, Brent. Welcome back. You're in time for a strong batch of freshly brewed coffee. You know where everything is."

Brent maneuvered around Tracy to fix his cup of coffee. After the first sip, he said, "You're the best."

His charming demeanor left the women in Charisse's office grinning and nearly swooning. The man had serious skills.

"I'm going to get to work," Charisse said, walking to her office. "Brent, I'll leave you to your own devices."

"Sounds good. Let me know when you want to go

over the interview with Gladys. I'll be heading out on a lunch appointment."

"Give me an hour to catch up on a few things. We'll meet in the conference room."

"Great." He hesitated before turning to her. "Is something wrong?"

"No." She walked behind her desk to keep the heavy furniture between them.

"Okay. I feel like I did something wrong." He stepped away, then turned. "By the way, the blue of your blouse against your skin looks great. And I'm still loving the shorter hair." He reached over and played with the back of her hair before his thumb brushed the rose tattoo.

"Thank you." There, he did it again. She groaned when he left, wondering how he could make her quiver with one touch. But all that would change when she headed to happy hour with June.

Charisse was surprised that she was able to concentrate and get through the various meetings with her staff. She'd even managed to vet a few nightclub managers for an upcoming event. As it got closer to the time that she'd meet with Brent, he began to seep into her thoughts with startling frequency.

"Hey, boss, got a moment?" Tracy asked, as she stepped in.

Charisse had wanted to push her talk with Tracy to the end of the day. Why have the sad news of her assistant's resignation hovering over her all day?

"Me, too, boss." Lance stepped in and immediately stood next to Tracy, as if for a united front.

Charisse clenched her teeth. For a day that had

started on such a high note, it was fast becoming a dismal one.

Charisse wondered if she should reach for the antacids before the conversation began. She kept her hands clasped under the desk.

"I'm listening," she said, her voice cracking a little.

"I'll go first," Lance said. His head twitched with a nervous tic. "Shelby contacted me while I was on vacation. She has her own company. And…well, she wants me to come work for her."

Tracy sucked her teeth.

Charisse remained silent. Her anger over Shelby's betrayal wasn't erased. Apparently her former friend had acted on her promise to take Lance.

"Miss Sanford, I couldn't do that to you. I like what I do here. You were the one who interviewed me and gave me a chance."

"What did she offer you?" Tracy asked.

"She said that I would come in as an assistant and then once I learned the ropes that I would be her second-in-command." His forehead wrinkled in consternation.

"Lance, I love having you on my team. You're an invaluable member of the staff. New Vision needs both of you. And I'm happy that you would consider staying here. I wouldn't take that decision for granted." Charisse hoped that Lance heard the sincerity in her message.

"Ma'am, thank you." He grinned, displaying shiny braces on his top teeth.

Charisse nodded. She appreciated Lance's loyalty. With so many changes underway, she was glad to have some things remain the same.

After Lance left her office, she turned to Tracy. With Lance's surprising statement, she held out hope that Tracy would also have good news.

"Don't you drag out the news. Did they offer you the job?" Charisse drummed her fingers on the table.

"Yes, they did offer. I told them that I'd need the weekend to think about it."

"That's good." Charisse opened the drawer and gripped the antacid bottle. "But the weekend is now over."

Tracy walked over and rested her hands on the desk. Tears filled her eyes. Her mouth quivered as she bit down to restrain herself. "This morning I called them with my answer. I said no."

Charisse took a deep breath, then blew out in a noisy whoosh. "I've been calling around for insurance rates. We had two more smaller accounts sign on after Brent's business. I'll be purchasing insurance that will help with your son's allergies. It won't be the best rates compared to a bigger company."

"I understand. Thank you for doing this."

Charisse touched Tracy's damp cheek. "We're in this for the long haul, my friend."

Tracy grabbed a tissue from the box on the desk. She dabbed at her eyes and nose, reddened by her quiet sobs. Charisse got up and hugged her. She imagined that they were both stressed over the situation and now they could move on, together.

New Vision had an excellent staff, a healthy amount of clients and enough friends, like Jake, who stepped in to assist. She had to make sure that she didn't take any of it for granted. There was much to do.

Chapter 9

More than an hour later, Charisse stopped her work and headed to the conference room. No one had interrupted her, even though she could hear the laughter and chatting outside her door. She hoped that Brent wasn't turning her office off-kilter.

She handed him the information on Gladys and waited for him to review it. "Gladys will want to interview you, too. Will that be a problem?"

"I'd prefer to be in the background."

"I would've thought the opposite." She kept her focus on the reading material. "Seems like you enjoy flashy entrances."

"I'll work on that."

"Not for me, please."

"What kinds of questions will she ask?" Brent ran his finger down the paper.

"The usual, like the background of the group. How'd

you find them? I think mentioning the funeral will connect with the sensitive ones."

Brent shook his head. "I don't want to play with people's emotions."

"You'll be sharing the truth. Don't exaggerate. Don't try to guess what people want to hear. Speak from the heart." Charisse appreciated Brent's hesitation, but she knew the business. "Pretend you're talking to me."

"I don't know." He shifted in his chair with his eyes downcast.

This was the first time that she had seen Brent unsure. There was so much to learn about him and what affected him. She didn't want to push him to do something he may not be ready to do. But hearing stories with resonance was what fans wanted.

"Anything else?" Brent prompted.

"If you aren't interviewed, we can at least send over some information in advance about the group. She'll probably create her questions from that information."

"Let's go that route. If I'm up to the interview, then I'll make myself available."

Charisse understood his reluctance to open up about his family life on national TV.

"I want to bring up another issue. The photographs that were taken don't really capture the group in the best way. These pictures don't show them as sophisticated, sexy, young adult males, who live for R & B. Instead it's a caricature of hood life, and I'm assuming none of them are from the hood."

"Again, what's the price?"

"I have a contact that will do it but wants exclusive access to them. He's starting out but wants to build his portfolio."

Brent nodded.

They ironed out a few more details before the time was up. Brent excused himself to get to his lunch appointment. Before he left, he rested a hand on her shoulder.

"I wish that I'd found you sooner."

Charisse rested her hand over the warm spot left by Brent's hand. She sincerely hoped that he hadn't felt the slight tremble of her body's reaction to his touch. Despite her doubts earlier, she recognized a real connection between them.

"Hey, you have a minute?" Tracy asked.

Charisse chased away the thoughts that were turning her body on fire to attend to Tracy. She motioned for her to come into the conference room.

"That job called me back."

"Yes?" Charisse now felt a chill.

"They made me a counteroffer. More money. But you need me here."

"I hope that I've never made you feel as if you owe me anything. You've stuck it out with me long enough. Your son is your priority. Take the job. Learn lots. Then when I'm the queen of PR come back with all the delicious secrets."

"You don't care if I leave?" Tracy cried.

"Tracy, I've been up nights thinking about you leaving. I count you as a friend and a great employee. I didn't want to push you, but I do have an offer." Charisse looked Tracy in the eye. "Would you be interested in a management position? You've already started learning the business. The clients love working with you. Shelby's loss is my opportunity. Take your time to consider my offer."

Tracy began to cry, escalating to a soft sob. "I need a tissue. I can't believe you're being so kind." She ran out of the room before Charisse could stop her.

Even Charisse had to bite back her own tears. On the one hand, she was thrilled that Tracy had had such a successful interview. On the other hand, her staff needed to feel vested in the company's success. There was no way that she could do this on her own.

Brent hurried over to her. "I was knocking. What's the matter?" He looked around the room, then patted himself down. "Sorry, no handkerchief. I saw Tracy running out of here crying. And you're also looking like the world is on your shoulders. I'm not trying to pry in employee relations, but what's the matter?"

Charisse waved her hand, struggling to keep her emotions in check and respond to Brent coherently. She wished that he didn't have that soft, concerned look on his face. In her emotional state, she couldn't be responsible if she broke down against his chest or simply kissed him.

The morning romp between them had not been discussed. She didn't know what to say. For now, she decided to set it aside.

"Tracy received a fantastic job offer."

He whistled.

"I know. The tears are happy ones, I think. I counter-offered with a promotion." Charisse looked up at the door. "I hope her response was a yes."

Brent pulled her into his arms and held her there. Or maybe she wanted to stay close. His embrace had the magic to dry up her tears. Her body switched gears, as she settled into the thick wall of his muscular chest.

Her hand found his heartbeat, steady and strong, beating against her skin with a hypnotic tribal calling.

She looked up at the strong chin that supported his firm, defined mouth. She wanted to feel his lips upon hers and stroke his neck with her cheek. A low groan rumbled in his throat.

He lowered his mouth to hers. She stood on tiptoe to touch his lips with a gentle, investigative kiss. His arms encircled her, closing out any unnecessary gaps between their bodies.

"I can't help myself," Brent whispered against her lips.

She kissed away his guilt. She wanted nothing to intervene with what she felt. For all she knew, she could be floating inches off the floor. Maybe it was the way he pulled her against his body.

She didn't want him to stop. His mouth seduced and toyed with her, coaxing her mouth into a frenzied response. Like a welcome visitor, his tongue entered her mouth with a tender introduction. The intimate meeting sparked warm rushes of excitement in every sensitive part of her body. Just like its master, his tongue charmed her at the merest touch and at its boldest thrust into her mouth.

Finally they pulled apart. Her lips pulsed as if they had a heartbeat of their own. She wanted to launch herself at him for an encore. But the longer they remained apart and the slower her heart beat, the more common sense began to ripple through, dousing any further flames of desire.

"I'm sorry," they announced at each other.

"Charisse…?"

She placed her finger against his lips. "I think we'd

better get back to work." Charisse knew they needed to talk, but not in the office. Besides, what she really needed to do was exit this situation, quick and fast.

"Yeah." His voice had a sexy huskiness that made her quiver inside.

She knew nothing about him. Yet her heart fluttered with a manic beat whenever he was around. Her body responded to him with a passion that she'd never felt. Even her brain couldn't stay on point, couldn't be rational and logical.

Charisse was suddenly afraid of what lay just around the corner. She hurried out of the office and bumped into Tracy.

Tracy reached out to steady her. "I was coming back to talk to you. Sorry I got so upset."

"No problem." Charisse avoided eye contact with Tracy when she heard Brent behind her.

She traced her lips with her finger, hoping that the lip color hadn't strayed to give away her actions.

"I'll get back to my office." Brent sidestepped around her.

She could feel him looking at her, but she refused to look up.

"I will take the offer," Tracy said, but her attention was directed on Brent's retreat. "I want to be with New Vision. Helping to build this company with you, Lance and Jo is what I want to do."

Charisse had hoped to hear this good news. She'd wanted Tracy to stay so badly that she'd been forced to act nonchalant. While the words stayed stuck in her throat behind the threat of tears, she hugged her friend.

"We'll do this," Charisse said, sniffing loudly.

Tracy grabbed a tissue and handed one to her.

Once they were both calm, Charisse said, "I've got to head out of the office."

"Everything okay?" Tracy tilted her head in the direction of Brent's exit.

Charisse didn't bother to answer. She'd have to lie. Even if she did want to lie, she'd have to use the right voice. One thing was certain: Tracy knew her too well to accept any offhand remarks. A blush started on her cheeks and shot to the roots of her hair. She couldn't let anyone pick up on her and Brent getting down and dirty. Instead, she waved a dismissive hand without speaking.

Charisse didn't know where to go once she left the building. Outside in the middle of the midday rush felt like a good place to be. She headed toward Leonard Avenue, walking past the rows of storefronts.

Nothing held her attention. People handing out flyers only irritated her. She grabbed the information so they'd leave her alone. Her pace increased to a brisk walk to distance herself from the vendors. Happily she weaved and dodged pedestrians and the onslaught of yellow cabs that mowed their way through the city.

She finally stopped in front of an Italian restaurant. She wasn't hungry, but she could at least get caught up on emails while she nursed a soda for an hour. Her phone rang in her hand.

"Jake? What's up?"

"I'm wondering why you're outside looking lost. My little lamb, are you lonely?"

Charisse laughed. She looked around at the small number of patrons and saw Jake waving at her from the back end of the room. She returned the wave and squeezed her way through the haphazard maze of tables and chairs.

"Didn't expect to see you here." Jake kissed her on the cheek.

"I wasn't planning to come here. Was taking a walk."

"You're six blocks away. That's more than a walk. What are you running from?"

"Not a thing. All is well in my world. How about you?"

"I've been stalking you for too long to know when you're lying. But I'll leave that alone. Did you get in touch with Gladys?"

"Yep. The interview will be tomorrow. By the way, I'm going to that brunch on Thursday with the young directors showcase."

"Haven't heard much about it. But I'm not paying attention to the local scene nowadays. I'm heading out to California."

"What meeting are you going to?" Charisse searched her memory for the usual conferences. Nothing came to mind for California.

"Another company has plucked me from my humble beginnings."

"Get out of here. You're leaving? These are your stomping grounds. Plus you've been with that company a long time." She paused. "So what are you going to be doing?"

"I'm heading up a division. And the position under me is open." He winked. "Get it—*under me.*" He chuckled.

"You're an idiot," she said, playfully bumping his shoulder. "And no, I'm not interested in working for you."

"Well, I'm glad to hear that," a male voice behind them said.

Charisse jumped. She looked up to see Brent glaring down at her and Jake.

"And this is?" Jake drawled. He leaned back, clearly ready to have fun with this situation.

"This is Brent, my latest client." She stared at Jake, hoping that he'd realize this was the same client he'd helped with Gladys. Plus she didn't want him blabbing anything.

Brent shook Jake's hand. Without waiting for an invitation, he pulled out a chair and settled in.

"Have a seat." Jake still hadn't removed the grin. Brent's mouth tightened.

"Am I interrupting?" Brent asked, shifting his gaze on her.

"Jake, who's a colleague of mine, was just telling me about his job promotion."

"And I'm trying to get her to come with me." Jake's grin got wider.

Charisse shook her head. Jake was definitely intent on being devilish. That didn't bother her, as long as he didn't pick up on any tension between Brent and her.

"That would be a loss," Brent said.

"I'm not going anywhere. I'm staying here." *With you.* The confession lodged in her throat, eliciting a cough.

"Uh-oh." Jake smacked her back a little too hard. "Hope I don't have to do the maneuver on you. I am certified." Jake winked at her.

"Jake," she managed when she could catch her breath, "congratulations on the new job. Let me know when you're having your farewell party."

"You know I'll have more than one." Jake stood. "You've kept me hanging out with you long enough. Brent, my man, keep an eye on her. She's my favorite girl."

Brent didn't return the smile, although he did shake Jake's hand. The day seemed to be continuing on a tipsy path. After Jake left, silence descended onto the table.

Charisse wasn't the type to say what was on her mind. Maybe all her years in the business had taught her to be diplomatic at all costs. Running out of the office had just delayed the inevitable conversation about what happened earlier in her house.

She had slept with her client, and she couldn't avoid the fallout forever.

Without warning, Brent reached across the table and covered her hand with his. She stared at his wide palm and long slender fingers. His muscled forearms were toned. But she knew every last inch of him was also lean and toned.

Wild, hot thoughts kept popping into her head: Brent standing naked in front of her. Brent kissing her breasts. Brent thrusting into her. She lowered her head to break his gaze. Yet she didn't pull her hand away from his. *Be strong, dammit.*

"Brent, look, I had a weak moment earlier. It's not in my…" She articulated with her hand what she didn't know how to say.

"Nature. I think the word you're looking for is *nature.*" Brent smiled and then kissed her hand.

She snatched her hand away as his lips touched with a scorching peck.

"I'm not going to play your game."

"Don't mistake me for a playboy. I'm not like that

character." He motioned with his head in the direction of Jake's departure.

She squinted at him. "No, you're certainly not him." She was grateful for that. "But I'm not him, either. I don't flirt outrageously, nor make sexual innuendos."

Brent nodded. "Okay, so you want to pretend that nothing happened between us?"

Charisse nodded. She'd like to pretend. The reality, though, blew up her rules. She couldn't dispel the images from her mind or numb the sensations in her body.

If she had the strength, she could pretend that, after today, Brent was a client like any other. That was a big *if.*

"I'll grant your wish," Brent said in a flat tone.

"Oh."

This is what she wanted. She repeated the thought to convince herself. Charisse tried to match Brent's detached manner.

"Now, I must get back to work." She took a cleansing, but shaky, breath.

"I'm heading off to some appointments. I'll give you your room. Tomorrow the guys will arrive in the morning."

"Good. I'll come to your office to meet them." She wanted to see him on his own turf.

"Looking forward to that." He shook his head and pushed back his chair. "On that note, I'm going to leave now."

Charisse chose not to leave with him.

Her phone rang. She glanced down at the displayed number. "Crap!" She'd forgotten that she'd promised to go out this evening. She reluctantly answered.

"June, hey, I was going to call you."

"I can hear you backing out already." Her friend sounded irritated.

"Yeah, I'm tired. Heading home early today 'cause I have a busy day tomorrow."

"Coward. Are you expecting a man to drop into your lap? You have to do a little work."

"Maybe I'm a romantic. A man will drop into my lap because I'm too tired to beat the bushes for one."

"Yeah, and the Easter bunny turns into a hot stud of man at midnight."

"It's been a hectic day." Charisse tried to reason with June.

After several minutes of going back and forth with June, she ended the call rather than listen to her friend rattle on about the woes of the single female in New York City. Her single status had never been a cause of frustration for her.

Putting herself on the market wasn't an option. Her career always came first.

Everything else came second.

Chapter 10

The hotel's wake-up call hurt Brent's head. He slammed down the phone and fought the temptation to turn over and catch another hour of sleep. The night had been spent tossing and turning in bed, replaying his gutsy impulse to seduce Charisse. He hadn't planned anything that risqué, not even a kiss. But seeing her standing there, looking fresh and tantalizing in the early morning blew his mind, not to mention his body.

What could he do now? Charisse had clearly rejected him. He wanted to convince her that he meant no harm. For her to think that he was up to no good unsettled him. Dating was new to him. Maybe he shouldn't have skipped ahead to such intimacy. But he believed that, with Charisse, fate ruled where common sense failed.

What he wanted more than anything was to figure out how he could overcome her objections and his own guilt for moving ahead beyond a casual friendship. His focus had to remain on All For One. Yes, he had lied that he'd leave her alone. A month ago, a relationship was the last thing he wanted. Now it was all he wanted.

At least he had a busy day to look forward to. All For One would be arriving in an hour. Admittedly he was excited to have them here in New York. Their exuberance would occupy his time and distract him from any tempting impulses.

Brent felt better once he was showered and dressed. He sipped his coffee on the way to his office and tried to sharpen his focus for the day. All For One's key to success was in this city. He and New Vision had to take control of their image. He hoped the guys had the stamina and passion for the ride. Thinking about the journey recharged him. There was much work to be done.

By the time he arrived at the office, the guys had arrived. Their boisterous horseplay took over the agency. His staff had gathered in the lobby to meet them. He liked the lively atmosphere. Their heightened energy had to be present like this when they had their interview later that day.

"Brent, my man, good to see you," Akhil greeted.

The guys greeted him, one at a time.

"Akhil, Kevin, Cameron and Archie, welcome to New York. How was the flight?"

"That little plane sucked, Mr. T." Archie shook his head. He looked as if he was reliving the turbulence, including the side effects. "I couldn't look out the window."

"He was like a little girl, just shaking," Kevin added, while staring at the receptionist.

It didn't help that the receptionist was clearly pleased with his attention. That hook up wasn't happening on his watch. None of these guys were twenty-one. He'd promised all grandmothers, mothers, fathers and even high school principals that he'd watch over them. Not that they made his job easy. But they had come a long way in a short time.

"Let's go to the conference room." Brent ushered the noisy group into the room.

"Brent, what was up with that trainer you got us?" Kevin asked when they got into the conference room.

"I want you to build up your strength and endurance for the grueling hours on tour. It also wouldn't hurt to look fit for photo sessions."

Akhil, who was the most muscular of the group, nodded. "I tried to tell them, but they were acting so goofy. You'll probably be hearing about it." He was the eldest. Brent had tried to get him to step up and be the leader of the group. But Akhil's shy, quiet nature tended to keep him in the background.

"You're a snitch." Kevin balled up paper and tossed it at Akhil. His pitch was off, and the paper bomb flew past Akhil.

Charisse opened the conference room door just as the paper landed at her feet. The room erupted in laughter like a classroom without a teacher.

"Okay, guys, can you quiet down so I can make the necessary introductions?" Brent said.

Thank goodness, they complied. Now all of their attention was riveted on Charisse. Brent couldn't help feeling a surge of energy at seeing her.

"This is Charisse, who will be handling your PR. As I told you, you'll have an interview later this afternoon on TV."

Charisse nodded along with him. "This is pretty big.

You want to be interesting and interested in what the reporter asks of you. Remember that whatever you say will have a longer life than you think."

Brent noticed that she addressed each member, talking directly to him. She had them in her hand. However, he didn't get the same treatment from her. Since her entrance, she pointedly hadn't looked at him. He even shifted his position around the room. But her gaze swept over him as if he didn't exist.

He didn't like being ignored. Did she have to be so good at it? She seemed to be able to turn off her emotions as easily as turning off a faucet.

"Brent, can I talk to you for a minute?"

He recognized her displeasure in the tightness around her mouth. He nodded and followed her out of the room. "What's the problem?"

"The clothes are all wrong. Do they have something else?"

Brent looked at the guys through the windows of the room. They weren't matching each other, but they weren't that type of band. A couple wore hip-hop style clothes, one had the preppy look and Akhil wore athletic gear.

"I don't want them to look like clones. They have their own personalities."

"I wasn't trying to do that. I'm talking about colors. This is their first time on TV. You need them to pop off the screen. I'm not talking about bright neon colors, just solid bold colors."

"Shopping now is not an option." Brent wasn't about to take these guys shopping in New York. Their budget would be in the red almost immediately.

"How long are they here?"

"A week. They have other appointments through the week."

"Let's examine the wardrobe. Maybe they can borrow each other's clothes."

"You must have bumped your head on the way over here." Brent laughed at Charisse's naïveté.

"Really? That's all you have to say? Move aside." She moved him aside with the back of her hand and entered the conference room.

Brent stayed near the door to witness the showdown. When she floundered trying to figure out how to bring order back to the situation, he would step in.

"Listen up, guys. We have a slight problem. It's about the interview."

"It's cancelled?" Kevin's voice carried his disappointment.

"No. It's on. But I have a suggestion about your attire."

"Yes?" Akhil sat up, his tone wary.

"One of the big things about bands is the visual connection to potential fans. No one gives TV time to bands with no name and no hype. So this time that you'll have on the screen is crucial."

"What do you want us to do?" Cameron, who hadn't said much more than hello, suddenly took interest.

"Let's check the clothing options now. You might have to make some switches among yourselves, but it's only for this afternoon. Think you can handle it?" Her tone sounded as if she was amenable to their objections, but her body language said the complete opposite.

There was a silence. Brent could have told her that the idea would tank. Borrowing clothes, yeah right.

These guys took great ownership of their style and clothing.

"We'll do it," Cameron said. They all nodded. "We'll go get the suitcases." They noisily left the conference room to retrieve their luggage from the lobby.

The conference room felt eerily quiet when they exited. Charisse leaned against the wall almost opposite him. She didn't smile, nor did she look at him. Her demeanor was completely relaxed. The way she had her arms folded across her chest topped off her victory stance.

"Try not to gloat," Brent accused.

"No problem. Then you'll owe me a gloating moment. Make no mistake, I'll rub this in."

He tried to think of a witty comeback, but his thoughts were interrupted by the guys' return. They lined up their suitcases against the wall, as Charisse had instructed. Then they opened them and sat back, waiting for her to inspect them.

Brent knew his own style and chose his clothing based on what suited him. But he wasn't about to pretend to be a stylist. He took a quick step back and decided not to select anything for anyone.

The task seemed to be another of Charisse's strengths. He enjoyed watching her sift through their clothes, pulling out various pieces, examining them and holding them up against their bodies. She questioned each guy to understand his style and the personality type he wanted to portray.

She looked up at Brent over the guys' heads. Her lips curved up ever so slightly.

Brent smiled back, grateful for her response.

* * *

As they sat backstage waiting for their time to go out for the interview, Brent thought he would throw up, pass out or rub the crease out of his pants. Why had he agreed to be interviewed? He had tried to back out, but had only earned a scolding from Charisse.

She'd stepped up and managed to keep the guys calm. They listened to her coaching tips, even role-playing with her. Whenever he made his suggestions, his voice sounded like a bear waking up from hibernation. His attitude kind of matched his crankiness.

"Are you ready?" Charisse sat next to him. Her gentle voice normally would've soothed the nipping of his nerves. But moments before a TV interview, nothing seemed to have a calming effect on his nerves. She patted his knee. "Try not to look like you'll upchuck on the hostess, please."

"I'm glad you came with us." He looked out at the set and groaned. "I think I should have a mint."

She opened her pocketbook and retrieved a small box of mints. He gratefully took one, breathing a little easier once he popped it into his mouth.

"Are you this nervous when you deal with contracts?"

"Every time. But I take the position of crusader. I'm there to fight for my client's interests, every single penny of them."

"And now…"

He had to think about it. What was so different?

"You're still fighting for your client's interests," she reminded.

"Now, I want them to be liked. Before, I knew that those managers wanted my clients. I knew they had bankable talent." He lowered his voice. "In this case, what if no one else sees what I see, hears what I hear? I know they aren't just another group of guys who can sing together." He looked down at his hands. "I feel it here."

"Don't let Gladys make you think otherwise. You can play to her, but let's focus on the masses of people watching. Let them fall in love with the group." Her face shone with confidence. She stood. "They're ready."

"I'm putting myself in your hands." He walked over to the guys and slapped five with them. "Let's hit this out of the ballpark. We've got work to do."

"And you know this," Kevin piped up.

They bowed their heads for a quick prayer, which Cameron led. Brent added his own plea for patience and protection. After they'd raised their heads, the production assistant approached.

"Let's go." Brent walked to the door but stopped when he realized Charisse wasn't following. "Aren't you coming?"

"No. I have to stay here." She shooed him from the area.

Brent didn't care that the production assistant, armed with a headset and clipboard, was hurrying him along. He grabbed Charisse's hand and pulled her with him. When she tried to resist, he locked arms with her and propelled her toward the cameras.

"She's coming on set," he said, deliberately using a tone that didn't invite discussion.

The production assistant raised his hands, as if in surrender or disgust. The young man seemed to have mastered the look of constant irritation. But it didn't matter to Brent.

He winked at Charisse and then turned his attention to Gladys. This time, when Charisse pulled her hand from his, he let go. The hostess glanced over at Charisse but zeroed in on him. Her deep-set eyes noticed his slightest move, as if sizing him up.

He remained cool. Time to bring on the legal shark instinct from his former life. This woman didn't need to smell blood in the water. Only he and Charisse needed to know how much he didn't want to be under the scrutiny of harsh lights and invasive questions.

She offered her hand in greeting. He'd expected her to shove it out at him, to show that she was the boss. Instead, she extended it as if she expected him to kiss the back of her hand.

His research had described her as a diva. Well, there were some other unflattering terms. There was some distant connection to European royalty through one of her marriages. She'd managed to keep the title as part of the settlement.

"Welcome to *My Lounge Show.* Good to have you here." Gladys's voice had a strong nasal quality.

"Glad to be here," Brent said, with as much conviction as he could muster.

"Today's guests are All For One and their manager, Brent Thatcher."

The guys waved and flashed toothy smiles. Brent stayed reserved, trying to anticipate the next few questions.

"Before I get to the group, I'm going to find out all about you." Gladys patted him on the knee.

Brent nodded. He'd been instructed that they'd go to a commercial break soon, and he'd leave so the interview could continue with just the group. The plan was fine with him because he surely didn't want to sit there smiling and nodding for an hour.

"Brent Thatcher, from where do you hail?"

"I'm from Boston."

"You may live in Boston, but I hear a bit of something else there."

"I was raised in Georgia, outside Atlanta."

"Gotcha! Don't try to come on my show and hide stuff from Miss Gladys." Again, she patted his knee. Her bloodred fingernails against her light skin were like danger signs to him.

Brent stared at the TV hostess, who had suddenly gone from conservative talk show host to comedic, down-home girl. The switch unnerved him.

"How does a lawyer making big bucks throw all of that away to manage a group that only sang in high school?"

"My education isn't something that is thrown away. I can use that education in a variety of ways. And I decided to now embark on this career path."

"So when you've got all the experience you need, then will you head off to something else?"

"That would imply that I've not found my path. But this path chose me when I heard the four high school students sing and then had them sing at my wife's funeral. Our lives intersected in a positive way and continue to do so with the people that I meet."

"I'm sorry to hear the sad circumstances of your meeting." The hostess seemed subdued. Her tone shifted to a softer note. "Before we go to break, can you tell us what song they will be singing today?"

Song? They had been told that there wouldn't be time for a song. He scrambled through his thoughts to find a song that they could do with no practice and a cappella.

"Ma'am, we'd like to perform 'One Moment In Time,'" Cameron said.

Brent acknowledged the save by Cameron. He turned to the hostess. "There you have it."

"On that note, thank you, Brent. Folks, we'll be right back." As soon as the producer signaled the break, Gladys leaned over and boldly stroked his knee. Her hand lingered too long for his liking. "How long has it been since your wife passed?"

"A little over two years."

"My Walter, may God bless him, just passed a few years ago. Hang in there. Life goes on." She hugged him, squeezing her body against his.

Brent didn't know what to do but slowly brought his hands to her elbows. This woman, who had only moments ago seemed ready to slice and dice him with her questions, had now turned into a soft and swooning admirer.

"Miss Gladys, we're back in ten seconds."

"We'll chat later." Gladys hurried back to her spot.

"Another woman caught in your web?" Charisse whispered over his shoulder.

"Do you count yourself lucky that you've escaped?" he taunted.

"Yes, I will write a tell-all book on how to survive your wily ways. And yes, I'll tell how to avoid getting sucked in by that smile." Her soft brown eyes glittered under the lights. Today she'd worn her hair in a tight ponytail, which he particularly liked because it allowed him to see all of her face.

"I hope you're not embittered by the experience. Will there be a happy ending to your book?"

"Well, I played a part in the conquest. But a woman has got to know her limitations. Kind of like ice cream. It might taste fantastic, but too much of it and you're going down."

"Pace yourself, baby." Brent hovered over Charisse's mouth. His desire had a penchant for coming at the wrong moments.

"Shh." One of the techies signaled to them.

They both turned away, but the sexual tension still lingered in the air.

By the end of the day, the video upload of the group's a cappella song had hit several thousand views. Brent knew his contribution to the high number of views was practically zero. The group's success was confirmed by the larger number of positive comments, along with the thumbs-up that the video received online. His phone buzzed nonstop with offers for other media appearances.

"Hey, want one?" Charisse stood in his office doorway with a beer in hand. "It's cold."

"Where'd you get that?" He walked over to take the welcome gift.

"I figured we needed to celebrate. I bought a couple on the way over here."

"Light beer?"

"Every calorie counts, especially since I had a great big burrito bowl a few hours ago." Charisse wandered into his office.

He watched her walk around his temporary office, looking at the black-and-white photographs on the wall.

Vicki had mailed a few items to decorate his office.
Charisse might worry about her weight and size, but she
was a vision of perfection. Her curves were well placed
and added, rather than detracted, from her femininity.

"How are the guys?" she asked.

"They got invited to a club by one of the local DJs."

"How long did the lecture last?"

"What do you mean?" His brow wrinkled as he tried
to understand her question.

"I know you sat them down in a row on that couch
and badgered them to death about what to do and not
do. Who did you put in charge?"

"Akhil." Brent was amused that she knew him so
well.

"You gave them a curfew, too."

"Yep."

"Good. They need boundaries. You've got a lively
bunch there. Yet they are good guys."

"See, I told you they have something special."

She drank from the bottle, and he admired her throat
as she leaned her head back.

"Let's get out of here," he suggested.

Brent looked at Charisse, as a tense moment passed
between them. He recognized the desire in her eyes. No
doubt, she saw the same in his. But it only lasted for a
second before they reined in their emotions.

"I should get home." Charisse set down the half-
empty bottle.

Brent didn't want her to leave. Yet he was afraid of
saying something that would make her run from him
again.

"You can walk me home."

He nodded. The way she bit her lip turned him on. "Give me one sec to call the driver."

"No. I'd rather have you walk me home. It's a nice night. I'm wearing comfortable shoes. There's no need to have a driver wait outside all night and into the morning."

Brent set down his beer. He didn't want to presume what he thought he'd heard. He remained silent but very willing to comply.

Chapter 11

"We'll have to take two subways coming from here." Charisse tilted her head at him as she played with her bottom lip.

"Not a problem. I'm not in any hurry." His body had a different opinion in its aroused state.

His hotel was only a block away, but he didn't want to interject anything that could kill the mood. "I need to finish a letter and send it out before I leave."

"I can wait." She slipped off her shoes before reclining on the couch. "May I?" She promptly crossed her legs on the arm of the sofa.

He nodded, almost becoming speechless as he gazed upon her long legs. Why should he be surprised that her legs were toned and gorgeous? He'd seen them before, wrapped around his waist. Somehow in his office, the effect was even sexier. What he wouldn't give to kneel next to her and trace the taut indentations along her calf muscle.

"I think you'd better get back to work so we can get out of here." She grinned.

"Yes, ma'am." He winked at her and returned to the work.

Typing wasn't his forte, but with the proper incentive, his fingers flew across the keys. Luckily he didn't have tons of mistakes after he proofread a couple of times.

Finally he hit the send button on the email. Then he shut down the computer. He dearly hoped that she hadn't changed her mind. Now she was lying on her stomach with her legs slowly moving up and down as if she was swimming. She flipped through an industry magazine while absently humming.

The roundness of her backside had its own separate beauty. The way the fabric spanned her form had a thrilling effect on him. Every time he admired her, he wanted to touch her. Skin to skin contact with her invigorated him.

The night was still warm, and there was even a bit of humidity. Spring seemed to be giving way to hints of summer. Brent pulled off his jacket and tossed it over his arm.

"What are we doing?" He pushed for a verbal commitment.

"You're walking me home."

"Like two high school kids after school."

"Maybe something a bit more adult than that." Brent offered his hand, and she laid hers in his. He walked hand in hand with her to the station. They had to stop and wait for Walk. He seized the opportunity to kiss her. According to the light, there were twenty seconds to indulge in pure sensual temptation.

He needed no further encouragement. His hands gripped her shoulders as he anchored her with his mouth. The delicious softness of his lips stoked the fire roaring in him. Her arms encircled his waist, searing their heat between them. Fully clothed, he still felt scorched.

Like the perfect dance partner, she followed his lead, coaxing and teasing. Their tongues spoke a language on a higher level, communicating with a mixture of the primal and the learned. And yet, the inner mysteries left to be uncovered in her filled his eager curiosity.

The light announced that it was time to walk. Reluctantly, he released her. Instead, their fingers interlocked to match the ardor of their recent kiss.

"Look, Charisse, I can't keep apologizing. I don't want to," he said. His groin ached for her, pushing his sanity to the limit.

"There's a time and place for apologies." Charisse kissed his cheek, close to his earlobe, and her breath whispered against his skin. "Tonight's not the night for one." She pulled back from him to look him in the face.

"Okay, as long as we have that straight." He could barely stand still as she hugged him and ground her hips against him.

"We're celebrating your success. I'm only sneaking a smidgen of ice cream."

Brent didn't want to be nothing but a momentary treat. He wanted more.

The light changed.

They stepped off the curb, and he was back in

motion at her side. She was difficult to read. Her sultry moves scrambled his brain.

"Do you have a problem with that?" She stepped away from him. "You've made it clear that you aren't ready for a relationship. I have my work as my first love. I think we're playing it safe to keep any heavy expectations to a minimum."

"So I'm like the other man?" Brent shook his head. She hadn't said anything that was wrong. But the reality hit him with a harsh stroke.

He played with her curl at the end of her hair. His mind raced with the possibilities of such an arrangement. Many guys hated clingy girls, but in his case, he wanted to be like Velcro against her skin. He was always the one to shy from commitment. Then why not play her game?

She walked away from him. Her hips moved with a liquid sexiness that made him hard. There was no doubt that he had wanted her. Even if he had wanted to be difficult and reluctant, his desire for her ruled.

He followed her, not trying to catch up but staying several steps behind her, to continue admiring her rear. He couldn't wait to hold her in his arms. This ride would drain his senses dry.

She headed down the subway, only slightly looking over her shoulder for him. The platform was nearly empty except for other night owls.

From a stranger's point of view, they were two people who just happened to be taking the same train. She sat on the bench, while he stood at the edge.

She leaned over and stroked her leg up to her knee and then down to her ankle. The heeled sandals highlighted her toned calves.

The train approached. She stood and walked to the edge, keeping the space between them. More people walked to the edge, blocking his view. He didn't have to see her to feel her energy.

He stepped back when the train doors opened and a few passengers disembarked. They walked on together, but she remained standing with her hand hooked through an overhead loop.

She faced him with a boldness that made him want to drop on his knees in front of her. Her blouse eased out of the waistband of her skirt.

Her brown skin peeked through the empty gap in her clothing. Another tattoo peeked above the top of the skirt. He'd missed that one. He'd make sure to take his time discovering all her body parts that had been inked.

They got off the train and then headed for another. Brent had had enough of the commute. He wanted to call his driver before he lost his patience. Waiting wasn't his strong point.

The ride was shorter, but since it was on a more popular route, more passengers got on the train. This time Charisse stood next to him. Her back molded against his chest. Her hip ever so slightly grinded against his.

His teeth gritted as he struggled to keep his hands to himself. He tried to keep his focus on standing upright as the train lurched at each stop. Finally, he followed her lead out of the station.

"Only one block left."

"You know how to make a guy work up an appetite."

"Makes it more memorable that way." Charisse blew him a kiss. "I thought you had more stamina with all those muscles."

Brent grinned, ready to take up the challenge. He walked alongside her, shortening his stride to match hers.

Arriving at the house by foot provided a different perspective of the neighborhood. The quiet street had a row of brownstone townhomes. As they approached her home, more and more passersby waved or called Charisse by name.

He didn't join her when she ran up the stairs to her door. His intent was to give her as much time as possible to step away from this moment.

"Why are you keeping me waiting?" she asked.

Brent looked up as she started unbuttoning her shirt in the doorway. He surveyed the area to make sure no one else was sharing in his moment. He ran up the stairs, lifted her into the living room and kicked closed the door with his heel. Déjà vu.

He hoisted her around his hips, supporting her with little effort. He walked up the stairs, oblivious to anything in her apartment. He wanted her, and that was all that mattered.

In front of the door, he paused. Crossing this threshold with her meant more to him. Could he abide by her rules?

She wiggled out of his arms and stood with her back to the door. Her hands gently cupped his face. Her gaze swept over him, coaxing him to follow her.

Charisse saw the hesitation in Brent's face. She wanted to erase his doubts. Gently, she kissed him, until she felt him relax against her.

"Join me in the shower?" She unbuttoned his shirt

and slipped it off his body. What a beautiful body, she thought.

"Thank you."

"I didn't realize that I spoke."

"Your eyes spoke volumes." He chuckled.

"Can you tell what they're saying now?"

"You're a dangerous woman. But I'm not going to file a complaint." He unpinned her hair and used his fingers to tease it loose around her face.

Charisse pulled her top over her head and tossed it on the bed. She turned her back on him and walked into the bathroom. She undid her bra and tossed it over her shoulder.

She waited for him as he walked up behind her and slid his hands along her body. Just the touch of his hands took her mind to a blissful place. She groaned as his hands slid along her breasts and cupped them.

Her body arched against his, allowing him access to the back of her neck. Like before, he traced the outline of her rose tattoo with tender kisses, paying homage to the symbol that spoke of her desire to be free.

Could he truly honor her true nature? Could she trust him?

"Come with me." She stripped out of the rest of her clothes.

He followed suit. They were so in tune with each other that their movements were almost synchronized. His gaze ravaged her body in the same slow fashion that hers was enjoying the length of his frame. Each thought the other was created like a natural masterpiece.

She broke free from his hypnotic gaze and stepped into the shower, holding the door open for him to enter. The showerhead and four jets on the walls soaked her body. The water beat down on her head and sides, massaging her until Brent took over with his touch.

Brent reached out and traced a line down the valley of her breasts, down her body to her belly button. His touch made her gasp and instantly retract, but at the same time she craved his touch so much more. It was all she could do not to beg for him to touch her in the most intimate of places. His hands knew how to bring instant pleasure, awakening her and quenching her thirst for him.

He gently washed her body, planting intermittent kisses along her breasts, along her stomach, on the apex between her thighs. She pressed her hands against the tiled walls. Her eyes closed tightly as she tried to keep control.

His tongue had other intentions as it delivered short flicks against her bud. She writhed under his grasp, and her moans couldn't be restrained any longer.

They didn't bother drying off as they stumbled and tripped their way to her bed. After the heat they had generated between them, she wouldn't have to worry about catching a cold.

She fell back on the bed, giggling in near hysteria. Her mind was drunk with his attention. Making love while under the influence of a dark, devilish, sexy hunk had to be criminal. Whatever the penalty, she didn't care. All she wanted was his continued attention, as she readied her body for him.

"One second." She reached over to the drawer near her bed. She pulled out a condom and tossed it to him. "Last time, you came prepared. This time, I'm prepared."

"I guess equality in all things." He rolled on the condom.

"Okay, enough talking." She pulled his head toward her face.

"I want you, woman."

"I'm here, ready and waiting." She slid her thighs apart and raised her hips for his initial entry. "Oh, my..." She gasped as her head arched back.

He kissed her throat. She was sure that she almost fainted from pure rapture. His chuckle tickled her skin.

Her legs hooked around his thighs. All verbal communication was momentarily cut off. Every slide of his body against hers raised the temperature, sparking flames of white heat. Their union worked on a plane where instincts ruled. His thrusts sparked an orgasm—and another and another. They both grunted in time with their releases.

"Don't stop," she gasped.

"Honey, you ain't seen nothing yet." Brent paused.

Charisse opened her eyes.

He winked at her before resuming his erotic motion.

As partners with a common goal, they reached one peak and pushed each other to climb higher and higher, moving like a unit. Nothing dared stop their momentum. They were at dizzying heights, breathing heavily. Their bodies writhed in sweet, delicious agony.

She wanted to be free. She opened herself to Brent and surrendered to the climax that exploded with tiny pinpricks of fireworks in her brain, behind her closed eyes, in her soul.

Brent didn't know if he had the energy to move. Morning would soon be easing over the horizon. He hadn't meant to stay through the night, but they couldn't stop touching and being with each other.

Daytime turned things around, though.

He eased out of bed, surveying the room for his clothes. After he dressed, he sat gingerly on the edge of the bed. He looked at Charisse peacefully sleeping, her dark brown hair fanned out on the pillow.

She stirred under his light touch to her bare shoulder.

"Hey, sleepyhead," he whispered.

Her eyes blinked rapidly. She stretched, displacing the sheet from across her chest.

Brent bit down on his lip to keep from taking her breast in his mouth. "I'm going to get out of here."

"You don't have to go." She touched his leg and slid her hand along his inner thigh.

"I'm trying to honor your rules." He restrained her hand, before he lost the ability to be the gentleman that she wanted.

"Oh, yeah, the rules." She took his hand and kissed it. "I guess it's time for the carriage to turn back into the pumpkin."

Brent smiled at her fairy-tale analogy.

"Guess we'll be seeing each other soon," Charisse said. "I think the guys will get some great press out of their interview."

Brent nodded.

Instead of taking the long commute back to his hotel, he called his driver. His BlackBerry had received dozens of messages during his escape with Charisse.

The guys were indeed a hit.

Calls for interviews had stacked in his voice mail.

He called his office to have his assistant start returning calls.

Back in the hotel suite, he took a quick shower, drank hot black coffee and headed to his office. His evening with Charisse already felt too far away. Reality had a way of pushing through all the fantasies.

His office, once again, had a festive air. Since he managed the operations from the Boston location, he wasn't always on top of the daily goings-on. However, he had been around long enough to know that this level of levity usually only came on Fridays, closer to happy hour.

Not even his presence as he walked through the small area seemed to dim the mood. He felt left out and went to the source—the conference room. As he got closer, he recognized many of his employees' voices, along with the rumbling voices of All For One. He opened the door and had to do a double take.

"Now this is a surprise." Brent couldn't stop staring at the guys. The young men sat clean-faced, neatly dressed, politely chatting with his office staff.

"Figured we'd show you that we were serious about this," Akhil said.

"And appreciative," Cameron said.

"You're the man." Kevin gave him a thumbs-up.

Brent was stunned by their transformation and honored by their compliments. These guys trusted him. He'd been filled with so many doubts, but they had finally gotten their feet on the starting position on the game board. Now harder work remained ahead.

"Heard there was a breakfast with a young hip-hop director this morning," Akhil addressed him with a questioning look.

Brent nodded. "I assigned one of the managers to go to the breakfast. As you may know, Charisse was also attending. Either way, we'll get the info." So they were keeping up with industry news. Charisse's talk with them must have made an impact. He was proud of them and thankful for her assistance.

He worked through the day, attending meetings and making new contacts. The work got his creative juices flowing and kept him focused. By the end of the day, he had booked the guys for a couple of late-night show interviews, and they would be opening up for a mid-level R & B group. The next step would require corporate sponsors. He had his work cut out for him. He sat at his desk, pondering his next move.

His phone rang, but he didn't recognize the number.

"Brent, I have your mother on the line."

Brent pressed the button. He tried not to worry. "Mom?"

"Hi, son, I tried calling you just now, but it rang out before going to voice mail."

"I didn't recognize your number. What phone are you using?"

"I called from my hotel. I'm here."

"Here? As in New York?"

"I would've come to your hotel, but I didn't know where you were staying. Your father is no help. The man couldn't screw in a lightbulb if his life depended on it."

"What's wrong, Mom?" Brent noticed that his mom wasn't getting to the point.

"Can you come over and have dinner with me? Or I can come to your hotel?"

"I'm staying at the Lincoln Suites Hotel. I don't mind

coming to see you for dinner." And finding out what exactly had prompted this visit.

"I'll come to you. I'm sure you've got a nice suite. I want to make sure you're taking care of yourself."

"Mom, I'm not a kid."

"I wouldn't know. Haven't seen you lately." His mom may be forgetful about the everyday things, but anything related to him was in a steel-trap box stored in her memory.

Brent sensed the lecture coming. Dinner would be a long event. He finished his conversation and hung up, knowing full well that he'd only managed to delay the punishment.

Once he was done talking her, he couldn't concentrate on anything else. He set the papers aside. His mother had something on her mind. But nothing he said would get her to reveal the information.

She rivaled any investigator when she wanted to know something. At this point, he didn't need her poking around in his life. His thoughts lit automatically on Charisse. No way that his mother needed to know about her. His no-commitment, no-rules arrangement with Charisse would not go over well with his mother, despite her own later-in-life rebellion.

Brent stayed busy, which was not that difficult when the Boston location had a flood of business due to All For One's success. By the time he left the office, he was the only one left. His staff had accompanied the guys to another event they had suddenly been invited to attend. He glanced at his watch, wishing that he had kept a keener eye on the time.

His mother was due at his hotel room around six.

He got to the room with only five minutes to spare. He surveyed the large space. He didn't have to worry since housekeeping had done a good job. Still, he wanted to make sure everything was in place.

A call from the front desk alerted him that he had a visitor. He provided the necessary permission for her to come to his room. Now he waited at the door, straightening his clothes and running a hand over his hair. Still, he tensed when a knock sounded at the door.

"Hi, Mom," he greeted. He hugged her, truly glad to see her.

"Brent, you look healthy. All those muscles look good on you." She swept passed him into the suite. Her head nodded as she scanned the room.

"Make yourself comfortable."

"I'll take a drink if you have one."

"Juice, water, soda?"

"No wine?" She made a face. No one would have guessed that she was in her sixties. Her skin was tight and without deep lines. Men complimented her, while the women asked if she'd had work done. Her hair, peppered with silver, was styled in a French braid down her back.

"You've lost weight." Brent's gaze narrowed on his mother.

She preened. "Glad you've noticed. I've been working out." She patted her hair. "Covering the gray when I get back."

"Is that a piercing?" He saw the small sparkle on her nostril.

"Yep. Hurt like heck."

"Okay, have a seat. What's going on?"

"I'm enjoying life and doing things that I've always

wanted to do." His mother's bracelets jangled up and down her forearm.

He almost asked what his father thought about all this, but that would have started an all-out war. Very early on, his mother had made it clear to the entire family that she would be no one's subservient housewife. Usually that came after a heated exchange between her and his father, who was more old-fashioned.

But this new person in front of him left him unsettled. The changes were dramatic. More important, he wondered what was behind the change.

"Do you have a boyfriend?" Guess he'd be the one to do the probing.

"I'm still married." She raised an eyebrow at him.

"But you're separated."

She grunted and waved away his prodding.

Brent sat opposite her, waiting for her to tell him why she had made this unannounced trip. The longer she waited to reveal her intent, the more he grew cautious. After catching up on her life of group trips to the casinos in Atlantic City and to wine country in California, their conversation dwindled.

"Okay, Mom, we've danced around the reason for your visit. What's the problem?"

She took a deep breath. "It's time for us all to be a family again."

"You and dad are getting back together?"

"Ah…no." She took a deep breath. "You and your brother need to reconcile."

"Did hell freeze over and I didn't know about it?"

The warm coziness of his mother's visit vanished. Deep-seated anger raged through his body, setting his teeth on edge.

"Stop being rude."

A knock on the door interrupted their conversation. Brent looked at the door and then at his mother.

The brightness in her eyes betrayed her thoughts. Cold dread shot straight down his spine. Was his brother out there the entire time? Did his mother actually do what he'd hoped she would leave alone?

He yanked open the door.

"Hey, Brent—"

"What are you doing here, Harry?" Brent looked at his older brother. He certainly looked worse than the last time they talked. It didn't matter. He didn't want to hear any sob stories. There especially wouldn't be any stories of reconciliation. His heart had tightened into a knot over the issue. His brother or his mother couldn't pry it open, even if they planned a tag-team scenario.

Chapter 12

Brent stood in the doorway staring at a face that closely resembled his. No forewarning, nothing, had given him a hint that his brother would show up tonight. His mother muttered her concern behind him. He ignored her. She knew that he wouldn't want to see Harry. He'd been clear on that several times in a major way.

"Brent, please step aside. We can't have this conversation in the hallway."

The statement didn't make him budge. Instead his grip tightened along the edge of the door panel. His vision constricted to the point that only his brother's face was the focal point.

His mother pushed him aside and pulled Harry into the room.

Brent didn't like the loss of control. "Look, whatever both of you have planned, forget about it. I have a lot of work to do tonight. And I'm not in the mood for this."

His brother had the good sense not to sit and get comfortable. Even though their mother coaxed him to take a seat on the nearby couch, he refused. His attention never shifted from where Brent stood on the other side of the room.

Brent noted the slump to his brother's shoulders. Harry, who was always a healthy size, now looked gaunt around the face. His clothes hung loose and rumpled. Where were the cocky attitude and the grandiose bragging that by now would've tumbled out of his mouth? No matter; he didn't want to delve deeply into Harry's current condition.

"Brent, Harry, I have seen this family ripped apart for a variety of things. Some need that friction to force out bad feelings and to generate love and compromise. This family doesn't need ugliness pulling us in different directions. I want this family together again."

"You keep saying that, but you aren't with Dad. So does this reunion only happen for some?" Brent asked.

His mother took a step toward him. "Stop interrupting me." Her sharp tone muzzled his next remark. "I don't know what ripped apart your love for each other. I don't care because it's not that important."

Despite his mother's sudden appearance for a family reunion, he had nothing further to say. She may not feel that he had a right to have his feelings. But he didn't plan on clarifying his actions. Harry knew why.

The memory of their last blow-up replayed in his head. The repercussions after that night lay heavy in his stomach. He didn't want to linger over the details. Putting distance between him and his brother helped to dull the pain.

Brent picked up his jacket, tossed it over his arm.

He shoved his hands into his pockets, his shoulders hunched close to his ears. There was no way that he could stand to be in the same room. His mind couldn't quite get there. The only release he could muster was to seek escape.

"I'll be back in an hour. Harry needs to be out of here."

"Brent, wait…" Harry's voice faded as if too exhausted to continue.

Brent didn't stop. Instead his pace quickened down the hallway to the elevator. He punched the button and stepped in without looking back when it arrived, knowing there was the security camera trained on the elevator cab stopped him from raging in the small space.

His parents never knew what caused the breakup. With his brother's penchant for not always doing the right thing, no one pushed for the reason. Well, no one except his mother, that is.

Loyalty had been abused and hopelessly destroyed. Harry had sat on a pedestal for a long time. From their teen years, Harry had been the born leader. Brent had followed him around in awe. Adulthood, however, didn't seem to be as kind on their lives. His brother's wilder and dodgier habits made it difficult to follow him. Instead of a younger brother doing whatever his older brother asked of him, their discussions seemed to end in frequent disagreements. Growing further apart, their lives went down different roads. Harry chased empty dreams. Brent got married and made plans for life with his own family.

Brent stood outside his hotel, not sure where to go. He had left his briefcase in his suite with the current workload, along with his cell phone. No way was he heading back in there. Instead, he hailed a cab. Moving on autopilot, he provided the driver with Charisse's address before settling back for the ride.

Etiquette dictated that he should have at least given Charisse a heads up about the impromptu visit. But he was without a phone, so he stood outside her door trying to make up his mind about what to do. Even if staying here was the plan, what would he tell her? She knew very little about his family and their craziness. Yet she was the only person he wanted to be around at this critical moment.

Although they hadn't shared the details of their lives, he still decided to stay. Maybe the comfort he felt in her arms drew him to be there. But it was late. And what if she had company? Brent's hand lowered from the door knocker. That possibility had never crossed his mind.

"Are you going to stand there all night?" Charisse opened the door. She wrapped her arms around her body firmly to keep her dressing gown closed.

"How did you know I was out here?"

"I heard the car and looked out. Couldn't believe it was you. Especially since I was thinking about you."

"I didn't mean to pop up."

"But you did, so come in. You look like hell. Is it the group? Don't overthink how well they did. Relax and enjoy it."

"The labels are already chomping at the bit. They're pushing for an early release of the single to ride the wave. Plus it looks like they'll definitely get on the summer tour lineup." Brent refrained from sharing the real reason he had ended up there.

"Oh, man, that is beyond fantastic." They hugged, celebrating the major victory.

"The guys are heading home over the weekend for a string of hometown events and appearances. I'll be heading to Boston for a bit." He raised her chin so he could look into those beautiful, expressive eyes. "Wish you could come with me." His impulses seemed to be on hyperdrive. He could only blame the night's events.

"Invite me."

"Okay." He kissed her gently.

"Here's my RSVP." She opened and dropped her nightgown.

All his recent irritations receded to the back of his mind. To be in Charisse's arms was a priceless gift. They made their way to her bed for a decadent night of pleasure.

"I can't stay, Charisse." Brent kissed the top of her head as she snuggled next to him. He stroked her shoulder, admiring how smooth her skin was.

"You know, I think the rules have been suspended," Charisse joked, poking his chin with her finger.

"Since we're practically addicted to each other, I kind of suspected that the rules weren't working. But I have to admit that I'm not leaving because of the rules." He slid his arm from under her head.

Being with her was like reaching an oasis in the desert. A minute in her company invigorated him. In her arms, while making love, was a natural high that he wished would never end. What he'd run from was still out there, even if his family had left his suite.

Charisse reached up and rubbed his bare back. "You're so quiet."

"Sorry." He reached for his clothes.

"You know I don't mind coming to Boston." She leaned back on the pillows, watching him get dressed.

"It's not that."

"You can talk to me," she encouraged. Something in his demeanor warned her that the matter was serious. She adjusted herself against the pillows.

"I had a bit of a blow-up with family before I came here."

"Your family is here?"

"My mother made a surprise visit and dragged along my brother." His face tightened as he began to retell the earlier episode.

Charisse heard the sordid details without interrupting him. An occasional eyebrow raised or a frown settled briefly on her forehead. As he wound down, she got dressed. He paused, waiting to see if she was really paying attention. Her opinion mattered to him.

"You've told me everything except why you are at odds with Harry."

Brent motioned toward the kitchen. "I'll tell you over a late-night snack."

"Good plan. I've got bread and deli meat. Mayo and other stuff are in the fridge."

Brent walked to the kitchen. The sound of Charisse's muffled steps from her bunny-shaped bedroom slippers comforted him. In a matter of minutes, he familiarized himself with the kitchen and its treasures.

"I like this. Feeding you." He busied himself with the bread.

"Feeding me?"

"Being with you, talking, standing in your kitchen preparing a meal. Makes me feel domesticated." He grinned. His words didn't quite convey how much he enjoyed being in her company. He walked over and kissed her. One hand cupped her head, as the kiss deepened with passion. His other hand balanced a slice of multigrain bread.

Charisse moaned when he stopped. She grabbed a slice of ham, nibbling on the edges. "I feel as if you're treating me to dessert before the main meal."

"Couldn't help myself."

In between munching on the meat and a slice of cheese she hoisted herself onto the kitchen counter.

"Babe, tell me about your brother."

"Harry worked a regular 9 to 5 job with the state as a computer specialist. Then he started with online gambling and then sports gambling. Before too long, he owed money. My parents helped him out until it got too bad, and then they shared the problem with me. Then I stepped in, picking up where they'd stopped, enabling him." Brent focused on adding the potato chips next to the sandwiches. His anger burned at a slow simmer.

"Is he still gambling?"

Brent shrugged. "I've lost touch with his habits. The last time he came to me, I said no. He begged, saying that his life was at risk. But I didn't budge. At that point, he wanted thousands of dollars."

"Sounds like he needed professional help."

"Whatever. Instead he went to Marjorie, pleading his case. He had to have the money that night." He looked up, but all he could see was Marjorie picking up her car keys. He'd asked her where she was going, and at first, she didn't want to say. When he'd pushed, sensing that something wasn't right, she'd confessed that Harry needed the money. She'd withdrawn it earlier that day and was taking the money to him.

Their fighting escalated with her accusing him of being selfish and uncaring about his brother before she headed out that night. A drunk driver and a thunderstorm took away his wife.

"Harry never got his money." Brent finished his story. He slid the plate toward Charisse.

She slid off the counter and took their plates to the dining table. "Come, sit." She offered him a tentative smile.

Brent sat, but his appetite had fled.

"I'm very sorry to hear about the sad circumstances of Marjorie's death."

He nodded. "Getting over it was difficult, but I've been doing fine."

"I believe that about Marjorie but not about Harry. You have to forgive him."

Brent clenched his teeth. The sandwich remained untouched. His mouth was dry. Eating anything would taste like sawdust.

"Right now you are at war with your brother, and it's affecting the relationship with your parents. Don't know about your sister, but I'm sure she wants a peaceful and quick end to the feud."

"A family is all I ever wanted. Now I've branched out to a new career, and I still want a family."

"I think that you can go through life doing all the things that you want to do. However, this will overshadow whatever you accomplish because you haven't completely let go." Charisse brushed his cheek with her hand.

Brent gazed into her eyes, sinking into their comfort.

What she said made sense. For the first time, he trusted someone who had captured his heart. For the first time in a while, he had fallen in love. The realization came at him like a one-two punch to the heart and brain.

He watched her finish the sandwich and brush away the crumbs. Now he had his own secret—one that he pretty sure wasn't the right time to share with Charisse. He'd fallen hard and fast for this beautiful woman with a warm heart.

"Don't try to make goo-goo eyes with me." She leaned over and kissed him.

"You've got your brother paying a heavy penalty. I think it's time to give him a reprieve."

"Can I think about it?"

Eventually he left Charisse looking soft and tender. They had talked a little about his strategy. Nothing felt comfortable. Why would it? Years had been spent blaming his brother and harboring ill feelings.

He left her with a soft kiss on her forehead. He heard her sigh and wished he had the guts to say "I love you." For that, he was sincerely sorry.

Having her in Boston would give him a second chance.

By the time he returned to the room and inserted his key card, he really hoped that he had the place to himself. The room was dark and he flicked on the lights. He breathed a sigh of relief that he didn't see his brother or his mother. His plan to reconcile with Harry didn't call for an immediate rollout.

After a quick shower, he slipped under the covers and turned off the light. Sleepiness hovered on the edge, waiting for him to calm his worries. All he thought about was how one part of his life seemed to be going well and another seemed to be in bitter turmoil.

He walked into the office the next morning ready to call a staff meeting. On the ride over, he'd made a checklist of all the things that needed to be done. The length of the list made his stomach nervous. Heading back to Boston was more urgent than he'd thought.

"You've got a visitor in your office." His assistant pointed toward his office.

"Who?" Brent stopped in his tracks.

"Your mother," she whispered. "She made me promise that I didn't text you."

"Did she also promise to sign your next paycheck?"

The woman's eyes opened as wide as saucers.

"Sorry," he mumbled. His mood, which was already dark with all that he had going on in his mind, now went south. His mother wanted to bring this matter into his workplace. He took a breath and proceeded to his office.

"Hi, Mom," he greeted tight-lipped.

"I figured that I wouldn't see you again last night after you threw your tantrum. I came here hoping that you didn't have a meeting so we could talk. Plus, I'm heading home today."

His mother had a way of knocking him down a size or two. And in this case, he had no defense. His fight then flight response wasn't cool. "Mom, I'm very sorry about last night. You know that I love seeing you."

"Liar," she joked, but her concerned expression didn't disappear.

"I owed you a good time when you came."

"Well, in all fairness, I dropped in without letting you know."

"And...I didn't expect Harry to be part of your visit. It was a big shock. Maybe with a little warning—"

"You would have refused me," his mother said, matter-of-factly.

"Probably," Brent hedged.

His mother finally sat with her pocketbook perched on her legs. She looked tired, despite the perfectly applied makeup. "When did we go off in such separate paths?"

"Life changes us, Mom. We outgrow things, have different interests and move on."

"All of that shouldn't destroy us. Besides, you haven't moved on. Holding on to Marjorie as your reason to stay stuck in limbo isn't right, and it's surely not fair to her memory."

"In a perfect world, maybe." His discomfort increased as his mother guided him down the path he didn't want to go. This heavy discussion was at the wrong place and definitely at the wrong time.

"You've never said why you and Harry don't talk to each other."

"Did you ask him?" Somehow he didn't think that when he shared the details with his mother that she would remain as quiet as Charisse.

"No." She crossed her arms and glared at him. "I expect that you are the one I need to ask."

Brent started talking, answering his mother's many questions. Every movement, expression, body language that his mother exhibited registered with him. She was already angry with him over the situation. He concluded his confession with a promise to make amends.

"When, Brent? You've exiled your brother for an unfortunate accident long enough. You can't withhold your forgiveness much longer."

"I know. I know."

"It's affecting the family."

"Mom, I'll do it when it's right."

"It's always about tomorrow with you. Unless you have divine power, you may not have tomorrow in your grasp." His mother's tone escalated. "How are we going to have family dinners at Thanksgiving or Christmas?"

"You've got six months to think of that." He glanced at his watch. Big mistake.

"Oh, am I keeping you? Your own mother and you treat me like a fifteen-minute appointment." She quieted, then looked in her pocketbook and pulled out a tissue.

"Oh, Mom, please don't cry." He knelt at her side with his arms around her. She sniffed into the tissue, dabbing at her eyes. His mom wasn't the type to cry, especially in front of anyone. Now he felt terrible.

"My birthday is in a few weeks." She gripped his hand and sandwiched it between both of hers.

"I know. I'm having a party for you in Boston. Dad said he'd host one in Florida." His mother was never the type to celebrate her birthday in a subdued manner. By the time that the day of the party arrived, he expected to have heard about at least two additional parties on her behalf. The woman was a born socialite.

His mother pushed him aside. She pulled out a small notepad from her pocketbook. "I'll probably have to take over your father's arrangements for my party, if I want it done right. Plus I don't want any of his silly girlfriends to get their hands on anything with regard to me."

"Dad has a girlfriend?"

His mom shrugged. "He's lost weight, dyed his hair, walks around like he's some senior citizen cover model. Probably a young gold digger looking to hitch up with an old fool."

Brent bit his cheek to keep from laughing. Despite his parents' separation, his mother was jealous. All her partying and having the house filled with people were acts to get back at her husband. His mother's logic always had a convoluted edge to it. He and his siblings had learned early on not to get in the middle of their breakup. After their first and only plan to reunite their parents that went terribly wrong, none of his siblings got involved or offered opinions. Yet he'd still call his father to see what the old man was up to.

"Mom, I promise that you'll have wonderful birthday parties in Boston and Florida."

"I'll hold you to that promise." She kissed his cheek. "I want my baby girl and two sons at the party."

"Where's Harry now?"

"He's headed back to Boston this morning. I bought him a ticket since he's between jobs. With all the good things going on at your company, I'm sure you could help him."

"Why doesn't he stay in Florida with you or dad?" Brent's plans to forgive didn't necessarily come with additional conditions.

"He wants to be in Boston. That's where his roots are, not with a bunch of gray-haired folk."

Brent suspected that she'd convince Harry to come to Boston. The role of big brother had changed, but then again, a lot in his life wasn't the same. Learning to adapt seemed to be the lesson he had to learn.

"Who is he staying with in Boston?"

"I got him a six-month lease in an apartment to give him time. But you know that it would be cheaper if both of you lived together. I'm glad that you did buy a new house because I think that it shows you're moving on, but it's too big for just you to rattle around in there. Besides, you told me that I could visit and decorate the place. I know it'll need a woman's touch. Talking about a woman's touch—"

Vicki interrupted in the nick of time. "Charisse is here."

"Mom, I've got to get back to work. It was good seeing you." He kissed her cheek. "I'll have my driver take you to the airport. And I'll definitely talk to Harry, sooner than later."

"Thanks, sweetheart. You always make me proud."

Brent escorted his mother to the waiting area. Charisse looked up from the magazine she was reading when he entered and greeted him with a wide smile.

"Good morning, Charisse."

"Hi, Brent." She nodded. She wore a sexy short skirt to show off her legs. He winked his appreciation of the gorgeous display that was just what he needed in the morning.

His mom paused. She looked down at Charisse with a speculative gaze before looking up at him. He tried to keep his face blank. The effort only served to cause a raised eyebrow from her.

"I'm his mother."

"Nice to meet you, Mrs. Thatcher." Charisse shook his mother's hand.

"What do you do for Brent?" His mother's question hovered ever so innocently.

"I work on public relations for one of his clients."

"Okay." His mother's tone left a lot unsaid.

The wheels in his mother's head were running practically on high speed. He cupped her elbow and steered her to the elevator. "Charisse, could you wait in my office?" He motioned with his head for her to go.

She remained seated, sliding back into the chair. Her mouth perked into an insufferable smirk. She didn't budge.

"Please?"

Finally, she relented and stood.

"I'm impressed, son."

"With what?" He pressed the button to summon the elevator and prayed it would come before his mom pressed him with intrusive questions.

The elevator arrived.

His mother stepped into the elevator and faced him. Excitement radiated off her entire body. "You found a lady to bring life back into your heart. I'd wondered what had changed about you. Couldn't quite put my finger on it. Has been a while since there's been life in those eyes. And now I know." She chuckled. "Charisse, is it? I like that name. She's as lovely as a sunny day. Looks like a nice young lady."

The doors sounded the alarm for them to close. Her delicate hand remained firmly fastened on the elevator door, keeping it open.

"Oh, and Brent…"

"Yes, Mom?"

"I want her at my party. I think that it's in my best interest to get to know the woman you love."

Chapter 13

After a week back in Boston, Brent decided that he needed a clone or two. Several of his artists were hitting their stride and gaining success in their particular niches. With All For One being added to the summer tour lineup, additional appearances and promotional work would be crucial to capitalize on the exposure.

The workload didn't lend too much time for him to talk to Charisse. Their separation made him miss her more. Though, he had to admit that she may have welcomed the space. Getting close to her beyond physical intimacy was turning into a difficult task. But he was up for the challenge, despite the niggling doubt eating away at his confidence.

Since New York, most of their contact was through emails and phone calls. Charisse had mounted an aggressive campaign with the group's social media network. Now she was on the verge of launching an updated interactive fan site with plans to have regional street teams that would act as a grassroots network to push the group's efforts.

All the work and success rolling in had motivated the guys in various ways. Some had even started considering having a solo career on the side. Others wanted to know how soon they could open for some of the top acts in the stadium venues. One of their suggestions that was floated for his consideration was to have a reality show about their journey to stardom. That one was nixed immediately. He didn't need this bubble to burst and cause any public backlash.

One thing the guys did jump on as a group fell under the category of vanity. They wanted to pose with rock-hard bodies on as many posters as possible. Rocky took his personal training services seriously, getting them on their way. On the first day, he turned into a drill sergeant with a boot camp workout that silenced their bravado.

All in all, the label shared their satisfaction with the sudden upswing and transformation of the group. Even Gladys approached him for another TV interview opportunity.

"Welcome back to the office, Brent." Vicki planted herself in front of his desk.

"Thank you. Good to be back, and there's much to do. Ready to put on a pair of roller skates? Things are going to be hopping for All For One. They're on the summer tour lineup. I need you to coordinate with New Vision on local media coverage. Charisse's taking care of all media, but I want you to work with her on the local front."

Vicki's mouth twitched.

"What's the problem?"

"Nothing. What else would you like me to do?"

"Plan a launch party to fall six weeks from now. Again, coordinate with Charisse."

"She might as well work in the office," Vicki said under her breath.

"Did you say something?" Brent pretended he hadn't heard Vicki's irritation.

"Nothing important. By the way, Francine Caldwell called for an urgent appointment to see you."

"I'm too busy for her." Brent almost cringed that the annoying woman had tracked him to Boston.

"She said that she has an idea that's already passed muster with her father. Because he was so excited about this idea, she wants to meet with you, as soon as possible." Vicki cleared her throat. "She's here."

Brent held up his hands to protest. "I do not have time for that woman."

Vicki snickered.

"I hope that you weren't talking about me, honey." Francine glided her way into his office. She was in a powder-blue skirt ensemble that may have looked decent on a teenager but was ridiculous on a grown woman.

"Francine, this is an unexpected…" Brent left the thought open-ended.

The woman brushed past Vicki and leaned over the desk to close the gap between her face and Brent. The scent of her cloying perfume hit him, and he backed up.

"I'll leave you alone," Vicki said.

"Vicki, have a seat. I'm not done with my meeting. Francine will have to reschedule."

Francine's eyes widened and then changed into angry slits. "I have unfinished business to discuss."

"Not a problem. You can make an appointment with Vicki, who can see you much sooner than I can." He placed his hand on the files covering his desk. "All of these have priority."

Francine stomped her foot. "My father sent me here."

Brent picked up the phone and dialed Caldwell's private number. He announced himself and exchanged the briefest of pleasantries.

"Francine is here, and I understand that she's got news for me. However, I won't be able to meet with her because I'm gearing up for All For One. The media are coming out of the woodwork for these guys. I'd hate to miss any opportunities."

"Don't worry about a thing. Francine's idea can hold," Caldwell said.

"It's not that I don't want to hear what she has to say, but I did offer Vicki to assist her."

"Bet that went over in a bad way. Look, Brent, it's obvious that you don't fancy my daughter. I tried to be an advocate, but even I know when to walk away."

Brent didn't know how to reply. It seemed that Caldwell was giving up, but he didn't want to celebrate until he knew Francine's next move. He ended the conversation with the older man.

"I don't want to meet with Vicki," Francine blurted.

"Because…?" Brent looked over at Vicki, who only shrugged and looked unconcerned.

"She doesn't like me."

Brent tossed down his pen and vigorously rubbed his face. "I don't have time for this, Francine. You need to leave my office."

"What about us?" she questioned in a shrill voice.

"There was never something between you and me. There isn't anything between you and me. Furthermore, I'm not available for the future since I am in a relationship."

"What? Who?" Francine's eyes grew wide.

Vicki's eyes practically looked the size of dinner plates.

"Doesn't matter." Brent delivered the message coolly. Thankfully, she turned and ran out of his office.

After several seconds, Vicki shifted in her seat. "Do I get to know who the mystery woman is?"

"No."

"Well, I'm sure Charisse would be delighted to know that you put up a courageous fight for her privacy."

Brent didn't respond. He wasn't going to admit to a relationship with a woman who wanted nothing of the kind.

Charisse made a quiet detour from the trip to Boston. Seeing Brent's mother had reminded her how much she missed her own parents, especially her mother.

Plus there were certain times in her life where she needed her mom's advice. Much had happened between her and Brent, more than she'd planned, and there was a high probability that much more would happen. She sensed that he wanted to push their relationship to the next level. But her deep-seated fears warred against the possibility of following her advice to Brent to let go.

The location of her childhood home in Rochester was the only familiar thing as she pulled up in a taxi. Eight months was the longest that she'd been away. Work had become her central focus, shoving everything and everyone else aside. Guilt rode heavily on her shoulders as she walked up the driveway to the bungalow.

The small stones under her feet crunched as she walked. The siding had been changed from the dingy white to an almond shade. The trees that spotted the front yard were mostly gone, and a low hedge now bordered the perimeter. The brown front door had been replaced by a forest-green door, to match the shutters framing the windows. A shiny door knocker displayed the family's name engraved in its center.

Charisse raised her hand to knock, but the door opened suddenly. Her niece and nephew appeared in the doorway, jumping and giggling. They called out to their mother.

They had grown so much. Their faces had matured, and the baby look had almost disappeared, along with a few front teeth. Her heart swelled with emotion that they were still enthusiastic to see her. She knelt on one knee and gathered them into her arms.

"Aunty Charry," they echoed.

"Hi, Tonya. Hi, Leo." She marveled at how her niece was now the image of her mother, Charisse's sister, and her nephew looked like her brother. She had flashbacks of that same face torturing her when they were kids. "Both of you smell like spaghetti."

They giggled. The evidence was the tomato sauce dried around their mouths.

"I'll take your suitcase," Leo said, pulling on the handle of her bag.

Charisse stepped into the house. A wave of nostalgia hit her as the smell of home-cooked food overpowered her. Once she told her mom that she was coming, the family must have organized a homecoming of sorts.

"Hi, Charisse," her sister-in-law greeted. She stood up with a noticeable bump to her stomach.

"Oh, my gosh, Maria. Oh, my gosh. I can't believe it. No one told me."

Maria chuckled. "I'm four and a half months. I wanted to get past the first trimester before I told anyone."

Charisse hugged Maria, then backed off with an apology. This longing to come home had been ignored long enough. She'd been afraid that she would get sucked in. Instead, she had missed obvious changes and transformations. She hugged Maria once more.

"Where's my mom?"

"She should be in the kitchen. I think she's cooking all of your favorite dishes. We're here for the food… and you, of course. And I'll pass up a day of cooking anytime."

Charisse laughed. She knew her sister-in-law had her hands full with the kids, and now, with a third on the way, she didn't have to guess how busy she'd be. The fact that she'd worked through her pregnancies and afterward was commendable.

She walked to the kitchen where the smell of food got stronger, and her stomach rumbled, ready to devour everything. The burners had various sizes of covered pots. The oven light was on. Then she heard someone coming up the steps from the basement. The door pushed open, and her mother emerged, laboring with several bottles in her arms.

"Here, let me take those." Charisse saw that they

were sparkling apple cider—the drink of choice for toasting.

"Charisse, did you get here earlier than you said?"

"No. Maybe you got caught up with this big dinner you're making and lost track of time." She hugged her mom and slid into the nearby chair. "I can't wait to dive in."

"I should say so. You look like skin and bones. Do you eat in New York City?"

"All the time."

"Probably drink all those highfalutin' coffees and nothing much of anything else."

Charisse shrugged. It really felt great to be home. She wanted to go to her room and get into comfortable clothing. Plus she wondered what had been done to her room. She pulled out her compact and surveyed her image.

"You'll be staying in the smallest room. It's now the guest room. I took over the room that was yours."

"No problem." For heaven's sakes, she was twenty-seven years old. Hanging on to her childhood bedroom was a tad adolescent, she told herself.

Charisse headed to the room that they used to joke was the size of a cell. The room could only hold a single bed and a chest of drawers. A fresh coat of paint and new curtains did brighten the small space, though. The chest of drawers was taken out and a space saver unit was now inserted in the closet. Being home was enough for her. She changed her clothes and headed back to the kitchen to visit with her mother.

"I miss you, child. Glad to hear that you were coming to visit. Made me happy." Her mom's eyes glistened with tears. She was the biggest crier in the family.

Charisse gazed lovingly at her mother. Lately, waves of emotions seemed to be affecting her in a similar fashion. All of a sudden she wasn't feeling so tough. Her perspective on a number of things had shifted. The future and her place within her family crept into her subconscious.

"Good to see you, too. The kids look adorable. You sure do know how to keep a secret. You never told me about Maria."

"Sometimes people like to tell their own business. But I'm thrilled to bits to have another grandchild in the mix."

Charisse didn't know if her mother was making any general references to her not having kids yet. But where her life was right now didn't lend itself to being a mom.

"Dinner will be served in an hour." Her mom smacked her hand. "If you pick, you won't want to eat."

"Just one," Charisse begged as she tossed a piping hot roll from one hand to the other.

"How long are you here?"

"Two nights, and I'll have to leave on Sunday. Need to be in Boston for meetings. I also may throw in a proposal for a British account. Pretty exciting, huh?"

"Sounds like your business is taking off." Her mother hugged her.

"I had a few bumpy moments." Charisse shared the details about Tracy and Shelby. "Then I got a lucky break with an R & B group. I'm getting a lot of calls since their PR campaign has made an impact."

Her mother celebrated with more hugs and kisses. Charisse helped her stir the various pots until her mother shooed her away to go talk to the rest of the family.

Charisse wandered through the house. The activity level had been subdued. She walked softly into the family room, noticing that Maria had fallen asleep on the couch. The kids were on the floor playing with building blocks. She eased out of the room and went in search of her father. He was probably in his room watching TV while working on a crossword puzzle.

She headed down the hallway, knocked on her parent's bedroom door and entered when she heard her father's invite.

"Hi, Pop." Charisse ran over to hug her father. More gray hairs had sprouted on his head, and his face had a thin layer of a beard forming along his jaw and mouth. Seeing her parents age was a bit disconcerting.

"Charisse, good to see you. I thought I heard you, but my leg has been bothering me, so I didn't come out there."

"Have you been to the doctor?" She watched him rub his knee.

"Do you think I have a choice with your mother watching me like a hawk?" He lifted his left knee and repositioned it. "I've got to lose weight, and there is some arthritis in my knee."

"So now you can tell me when it's going to rain?" Charisse joked.

"I probably would be more accurate than those lame weather people on TV." He patted the bed for her to sit.

She slid into the side where her mother slept and propped the pillows to make a comfortable backrest.

"When are you retiring, Dad?" She remembered his vow when he was younger saying that they would have to carry him out before he retired. He was the classic workaholic. Many of her activities, games and spring vacations had passed without her father's attendance.

"I may not have a choice." His tone turned bleak. "Early retirement options are being presented to everyone at the plant. Doesn't make sense for me to pass it up." His shoulders hunched. His shirt looked a size too big.

Charisse worried that not having a purpose each day could adversely affect her father's mood. For many years, going to the plant was his life. Now he had to readjust against his will. He might find that home life wasn't his thing. She'd have to talk to her mother about her concerns.

"Fill me in on what's happening with you. You're looking like those fancy-dressed city girls. But you don't need all that makeup."

Charisse settled back against the pillows. Now this was the father that she was used to, reminding her that she was his little girl. She updated her father until her mother called out to announce dinner.

Chapter 14

By the end of the evening, Charisse had reconnected with her family, including her brother when he came to get Maria and the kids. Seeing her brother opened up the floodgates to a chatty reunion. She had much to share.

"Tomorrow morning, will you come walk with me?" her mother asked.

"Sure." Charisse hadn't brought workout clothes, but she could wash a load before she headed off to Boston. "I'm going to head to bed now."

In her small room, Charisse relaxed on the bed. She called Brent, once more. From the time the plane landed to now she had placed several calls. All had gone to his voice mail. She understood that he was probably busy. Yet she wanted to hear his voice, listen to him flirt and conjure up all kinds of hot, steamy thoughts about them.

She called once more, this time leaving a message. "Brent, it's Charisse. Wondering what you're doing right now. I'm at my parents' home. Now I'm heading for bed. Miss you…um, goodbye." *I love you.*

She held the phone under her chin. Her eyes closed over the silent confession. Had coming home stripped away all her final defenses?

She cringed at sounding wimpy. First, she had blabbed about missing him. Now she couldn't stop thinking about his face, his touch, his voice, everything about him. No one had ever made her feel so soft and vulnerable. She wished she could go back and delete her message. All that effort to stay strong and detached had been an epic failure.

Just in case Brent did call, she slid her cell phone under her pillow. The setting was on vibrate and at the loudest ring. She didn't want to miss his call or text.

Charisse groaned. She blindly reached for her cell phone. The sun poured through the sheer curtains, piercing through her slightly opened eyes. She'd have gladly closed her eyes again, if only her phone would stop ringing.

"Hello," she croaked, sounding as if she'd been bar hopping all night.

"I'm waiting for you, sweetheart." Her mother's energy bounced through the phone as if she'd loaded up on a gallon of strong coffee.

"Coming." Charisse hung up and lay in bed for a bit. Gradually the memory resurfaced that she'd called Brent before falling asleep. Although she doubted that she'd missed hearing his call, she checked her phone.

Disappointment didn't sit well first thing in the

morning. She dragged herself out of bed to avoid having her mother summon her with another phone call.

The scent of coffee greeted her. Her mom already had a mug and was sitting on the deck. Charisse helped herself and joined her mother. The sun highlighted her mom in a wide brush of light.

"I love the color, Mom."

"It's called sienna." Her mom ran her hand over hair that was pulled into a ponytail. "Slowing down the clock."

"Is that why you're doing this?"

"Yep, to stay fit." Her mother finished tying her walking shoes. "Besides, I figured that we could talk without having to deal with interruptions."

Charisse nodded.

"I can feel that you've got yourself tied in knots over something. I'm still a good listener. It's why you came home, right?"

Charisse nodded, again. Her mom was the best.

They headed out into the neighborhood. Other women walked or jogged along the same sidewalk. Charisse didn't recognize any of them. It looked like the neighbors had also changed.

Walking through the winding streets, shaded by large oak trees, was a stark contrast to the busy concrete labyrinth of the city. Even the air smelled different. She could bet that if she stayed there long enough, the daily stress of her life would ease away. But it was that stress that excited her.

Shoulder to shoulder, Charisse and her mom walked together. The sun warmed the early morning enough to make her sweat after the first block. She should have brought a water bottle.

Her mother pointed down the street. "We'll walk through the neighborhood to the shopping center and back."

Charisse listened to her mom act as a tour guide through the area. She learned who had recently moved in. Her mother pointed out those who didn't mow their lawns unless the housing association came after them. Since young families had replaced the empty nesters, a new playground had been added to the other end of the community.

Her phone vibrated against her side. She looked at the display. Brent. Finally.

She promptly answered. "Hey." She smiled, happy to hear his voice.

"You called? Sorry I missed it. Cameron had a birthday bash. I'm too old to hang with these guys."

"I think you're just fine. I've seen you in action," she said in a softer tone, falling back a few paces from her mom.

"I'll be sure to keep myself limber for you."

"Promises, promises."

"How's your visit home?"

"You know, I think it was a good time to visit and reconnect. I have your mom to thank for this."

"My mom? Did she call you?"

"Calm down. No, she hasn't called me. I saw her in your office with you standing right there." Charisse hesitated to get across her point. "Your mom is so proud of you. She cares about what you're doing. I think she worries a lot about you, too. From what you shared with me, she worries about all her children to the point where she'll intervene. I know that I've been holding off coming home because of work and stuff.

So thanks to your mom, I wanted to come home and be with mine." Great. She'd done it again, running away with the touchy-feely stuff.

"She'd love to hear that she had that effect on you," Brent replied.

"Good. I'd love to tell her one day." Charisse bit her lip. Why couldn't she filter her thoughts? Before he could reject her request, she piped up. "I have to run, literally. I'm walking with my mother."

"Sure. Can't wait to see you in a few days."

"Bye." She stared at the phone for a few seconds before returning it to her hip.

Talking to Brent gave her a burst of energy. She felt charged all over. Her desire to be with him overwhelmed her with its intensity. She sucked in air, wondering how to cure her need for him without committing.

"Coming, Charisse?" Her mother had continued on but now stood waiting for her at the crest of a hill.

Charisse used the adrenaline rush from her conversation with Brent to motivate her as she jogged to her mother.

She apologized when she finally reached her mom. Her breath came a bit more labored than she'd have liked. It was time for her to get in a gym on a regular basis.

"A new friend?" Her mom wiggled her eyebrows, causing both of them to laugh.

"Kind of."

"A sort of boyfriend?" Her mother gently pushed. "Care to share any details?"

"Details are up in the air. Not sure what to share."

Charisse followed her mother through the small

winding roads that led to the shopping center. The journey matched the curvy road that she was on with Brent.

"I set the rules for it," Charisse volunteered.

"I'm glad that you're strong enough to set your boundaries. But why did you feel the need to do so?"

"I don't want to feel that I'm not in control. Dating is fine, but then marriage follows and the rules change. A lot of these guys say that a woman who works doesn't bother them, that they want such a woman. But when the work is still a priority for the woman, they get huffy. My work is my life. I've been preparing to have my own business my whole life."

Her mother nodded but remained silent.

"Brent and I have our boundaries."

"What's the problem?"

"I've fallen in love." Charisse kicked a rock out of the way. Dammit, how could she fail by her own rules?

"And that's a curse?" Her mother pulled her to stop. "Since when do you run from life? Life isn't only about working and making money. It's not about having a house and the best clothes that money can buy. You still need someone to share these things with, whether it's a boyfriend, a daughter, or a pet."

Charisse refused to respond. She understood what her mother was saying and she didn't necessarily disagree with it. But the timing of this sudden turn in her still very new relationship rattled her nerves.

The rest of the day Charisse stayed on safe subjects with her family. She caught her mother's eye over dinner. Immediately after the meal was over, she popped up to volunteer to load the dishwasher.

"Living life takes courage, Charisse." Her mother

set the dirty dishes in the sink. "I know you have it in you to do what's right for you."

"That would make one of us."

By Sunday, Charisse was ready to head off to Boston. She'd gotten the comfort she needed from being around her family and catching up with her niece and nephew. It was time to head back to reality.

She pulled her suitcases into the living room. Her flight wasn't until that evening, but she didn't want to wait until the last minute to get her things together. Besides, the tasks gave her something to do rather than deal with her mother's sadness that she was leaving again. She had to promise not to stay away too long to stem her mom's tears.

Charisse went in to her parents' room to talk to her father before she left.

"Dad, are you going to come out today? You can't stay in here and numb your mind on the TV all day."

"I'm fine."

"None of us are. We need to see your face. At least let me beat you in a game of bid whist," Charisse coaxed.

Her dad chuckled. His eyes crinkled at the corners. She knew that she had reached him when he turned to look at her.

He asked, "Will you stay for dinner?"

"I can't. I have to fly out to Boston. I have to work."

"And to see that guy?"

"Mom told you." She cupped her face as it warmed. Her father knew that she had lost her mind over a guy.

He nodded. "Not that I asked but she couldn't stop

prattling on about it." He swung his legs to the side and got up slowly. "Now that felt good."

"I'm glad." She hovered nearby in case he needed her. But he gingerly made his way to the door. She was happy to see him get up. Her father had a fighting spirit that needed to be encouraged.

For an hour, she played cards with her parents and one of their neighbors who visited. Charisse didn't know what overcame her. Their soft laughter felt like a cozy blanket of security. The scent of banana bread reminded her of her childhood and of her mother's calming presence in her often angst-ridden life.

Family had seemed like something that she could set aside and wait to happen. But her family had never put her aside. Her guilt pushed against her emotional limit, and she felt the urge to cry.

After one of those sentimental waves hit with an unexpected impact, Charisse had to excuse herself from the table. She had to pull herself together in the bathroom. The tears had been reigned in through the weekend and now couldn't be controlled. She stared at her reflection.

"Get it together," she whispered between clenched teeth. She kept wiping the tears that spilled, which was an open invitation for more to follow.

A knock on the door startled her. She turned on the faucet to drown out the sound of her blowing her nose. "One sec."

"Are you okay, honey?" her mother asked in a soft voice.

"Yeah." Charisse splashed her face with cold water. She tried to blink the redness out of her eyes. Even fanning her face didn't help.

Finally she opened the door, keeping her gaze down. Her mother was nowhere in sight. Good. Her emotional breakdown could remain out of sight, tucked away and hopefully buried.

"Charisse, could you come in a second?"

"Mom?" Charisse pushed open the door that was once her old bedroom door. Beyond the doorway, she might as well have stepped into another world.

The room that was once mint-green now was a soft honeydew color. Not much furniture was in the sizable room. The wallpaper and random celebrity posters had been replaced with framed paintings and sketches.

Her mother watched her as she examined each framed picture. The paintings varied from vast landscapes to bowls of colorful fruit. A few featured a playground with young children and silhouettes of individual people. The sketches were in pencil, but the paints were oil-based with vivid color. It wasn't until she reached the last frame that she leaned in to read the signature.

"Mom, this is you?" Charisse turned to face her mother.

Her mother nodded. She looked as if she was going to burst with excitement.

Charisse was truly amazed. She had to look at her mother because what she saw in this room exposed a woman she didn't know. Her mother wore a smock with paint spattered all over it. Off to the side was her easel with a work in progress.

"When did you do all of this?" Charisse asked.

"I started over a year ago. Had to take a few classes to get my head back in the game. Didn't take long, though. These are all for practice. I'm trying to find the right thing."

Charisse walked around the room again, surveying all the works. She shook her head. "This stuff is good."

"Thanks, daughter, but a reviewer may not feel that way."

Charisse shrugged. "Who cares what some snobby wannabe artist thinks?"

Her mother laughed heartily. She walked over to her sketch pad and took a seat.

Charisse took a seat opposite her on a bar stool. Her mother flipped over to a clean page on the easel. Her hand flew across the page, and only the sounds of the pencil against the page could be heard.

"Stop making that face," her mother admonished. "You're messing up your jawline."

"I don't want a portrait," Charisse replied, although she wanted to see her mother's drawing. "Mom, is painting what you're doing now?"

"I'm switching gears. I'm not needed as much in one part of my life. Now I can feel free to pick up my aspirations."

"Seems like the woman always has to put her life aside."

"Is that what you believe?" Her mom's brow furrowed into deep creases.

"It's what I saw all my life." Charisse tried to remove any signs of complaint from her statement.

"Then child, you only saw what you wanted to see." Her mother shifted her position from behind the easel. She set down the pencil. Clearly, she wasn't pleased.

"Uh-oh, I feel a lecture coming on." Charisse slid

off the bar stool. She wanted to leave but knew better than to walk out on her mother's scolding.

"I'm not going to tell you what you know I'll say. Instead, I'm going to let you come to your decision. You're smart, a bit of a control freak, but you have a good heart."

Charisse felt that her heart was still up for debate. So far, it had taken her on a giddy ride. If she followed its wish, the outcome might turn her world upside down. She didn't want to ever feel regret if things turned sour.

"Stop being intense. Live your life."

Charisse stared at her mom. "I am living my life. That's the problem."

"Don't be hard on yourself. Great that you made rules. But it's okay to open the gate and walk through unfettered."

"Sounds like your drawings bring out the poet in you."

"I do nurture my artistic side. Helps with my painting."

"My PR business is what I'm nurturing."

"You're not one-dimensional." Her mom's fist hit her open palm with emphasis. "You can't starve one part of you. Eventually it does affect the other part of your life."

"I think if a partner can't understand what is important, then they don't belong in your life."

"You paint quite an idealistic picture. You leave no room for compromise. And you don't bring the right balance of color to your life."

Charisse tried to shake off her mother's judgmental remarks. She didn't want to argue anymore. Time to put things into motion so that she didn't get off the path of her dream.

Chapter 15

Charisse sat on the corporate jet still feeling disoriented. Her seat belt was securely fastened around her waist. She'd said several prayers. Yet her hands gripped Brent's arms every time the plane hit an air pocket.

"I've got one of the best pilots. Don't worry." Brent looked relaxed and sexy in casual clothes.

"Why did I let you talk me into this? I'm pretty busy." Charisse couldn't get over Brent's penchant for surprising her.

"I wanted to give you a ride in my jet. We've done the town car often enough. And I want to take you on a special lunch date."

"It had better be good food."

"I have no doubt that you'll be impressed."

Impressed was an understatement. She squirmed in the plush leather seat. "Why do we have to eat in Tennessee?"

"You'll see." Brent looked at his watch. "We'll land in about thirty minutes."

Charisse released his arm. She wanted to take a few minutes to spruce up her face. Since they were arriving in Tennessee in style, she had to look decent.

The restroom on the plane was only slightly bigger than the one on a commercial airline. Charisse made do with the small space as she retouched her makeup. She looked at her reflection and hoped that her red dress with black trimming was classy enough for whatever they would be doing.

Before long, the plane landed at the Knoxville Downtown Island Home Airport. Charisse hopped off the plane, happy to touch solid ground.

"Welcome to Knoxville, Ms. Sanford, Mr. Thatcher."

"Randy, good to see you."

Charisse followed Brent's lead and shook the young man's hand. Now she was really curious.

They walked away from the plane as a black limo appeared. Charisse looked at Brent, who grinned. She couldn't see his eyes because of his dark, black-framed glasses. As soon as the limo door closed, she turned toward him.

"What is going on?"

"Are you familiar with car racing?"

She nodded.

"We're on our way to meet Marc Newton."

"The race car driver?" She didn't know a thing about the sport, but Marc Newton was one of the few African-American drivers making headway in the ranks. Plus he was a definite cutie.

"You can erase that smile. I'm not here for you to go

all goo-goo over him. This is a little bit of work mixed in with the pleasure of your company."

"Listening," Charisse quipped. Wariness crept into her thoughts.

"The Newton team wants to shift their PR campaign. They are shopping around."

"And…" Charisse's pulse sped up.

"I told him about your services. We're skipping over his management people and talking directly with him."

"How did you manage that one?"

"I met him at a charity event. He is a great guy. We've become friends over the years. After we're done talking, we can head out for lunch."

Charisse needed a moment to digest the information. Having a client at that celebrity caliber would give her company a boost that no advertisement could do.

"What's the matter?" Brent asked. "No need to worry."

"I don't have the capacity to deal with such a company's needs." Charisse hated having to admit such a weakness.

Brent took her hand between his. Although he smiled at her, Charisse sensed that something crucial was about to be said.

"While you listen to Marc and what he needs, don't worry about how you will manage this. I have a proposal."

"Spill."

"Well, I was going to wait until you'd talked to Marc."

"Nope. You're going to tell me everything, or else I'm not meeting Newton." She said the statement with as much strength as she could muster. Speaking with such bravado would only work when the famous race car driver wasn't in front of her. Her excitement would be uncontainable if she did land the deal.

"He's got a huge campaign in mind—one that would require major capital and labor."

Charisse tried to beat back the panic.

"I can help. My offer is to merge our businesses." He turned to look out the window. "I really wanted to wait until you'd talked to Marc."

Charisse felt like the world had just stopped. Blood rushed through her body at an accelerated pace. Heat suffused her face as her emotions peaked.

"Marc's consideration of your company is separate from my offer. But whether it's Marc's business or some other company, I only see a win-win situation if we merge efforts. I would be offering you the ability to go after bigger clients."

Charisse nodded. She still didn't know what to say. In the meantime, her head kept rocking like a bobble-head doll.

The ride was spectacularly short. When she emerged from the limo, several people greeted them. Their smiles were too wide, teeth too bright. Her hand was pumped in hearty handshakes. Their voices intermingled and sounded like gibberish. Her brain fought to make sense of it all, needing more time to analyze.

"Don't look so petrified," Brent whispered in her ear. His hand against her back did comfort her.

Charisse didn't say much as she took in her surroundings. She entered Newton's management office. The one-story, crisp white building had the outward appearance of a warehouse. Once she entered the doors, the cool interior was a beehive of activity.

She greeted more of the staff. Many knew Brent, who lagged behind to catch up with them. Charisse continued following one of the employees into a conference room.

For one second, she wanted to be just a fan. Marc Newton stood in the living flesh. The man had a slim athletic build and a drop-dead gorgeous face. He could certainly have a dual career as a model for fitness gear. Her mind was already running through the possibilities.

Charisse listened carefully to what Marc needed. Endorsements were already coming in. But he also wanted more PR for a few charity events, which surprised her.

"I'm interested in cystic fibrosis and childhood diabetes."

"Is there a personal connection?"

"Yes. My niece has cystic fibrosis and a friend's son has diabetes. I want to use my celebrity status to push two massive fundraisers."

"Sounds like you also need an event planner." Charisse aimed to find out everything that Marc would need.

Brent entered the room. The reunion of the two friends halted further discussion for several minutes.

"What do you think of Charisse?" Brent looked at her with a big grin.

"We're just getting started. I have a couple of charity jobs that I would want her to promote. Also, this is the time to starting thinking of what endorsements I should have my name attached to."

"Marc, since I only learned of this meeting within the last hour, I will need time to let everything sink in. What's your time frame for a response?"

"I'll give you all the time you need. The charity events have to be done in the summer, though."

Charisse collected as much information as possible. She had already accepted the job in her mind.

"Do you have plans for lunch?" Marc asked.

"I'll take Charisse to lunch. Any recommendations?" Brent looked at her.

"I own a restaurant in downtown Knoxville. You have to come try it." Marc waved away her objections.

Soon they were in the private dining area of a very busy Tennessee restaurant. Charisse concentrated on the menu, trying to block out the lunchtime chaos. Otherwise, she would read the oversize menu and still not pick anything. But how could she stay focused when Brent had dropped the bomb of a possible merger with his company?

They ordered their food. No conversation unfolded for a few minutes. They nibbled on the warm rolls at the table.

Finally Charisse spoke, "Why would you make such an offer to me? Mixing business with what we have… well, it makes me uncomfortable."

"I hope that what we have is worthy of giving it a name. I know that we have a future, and I think we should work toward something that is more long-term and solid. My feelings aren't wavering."

"Really?"

"Yes, really. How about you? Tell me what's in your heart."

"I like what we have. But I can't stop in midstream with my business."

"That's why if we merge, you won't have money issues to hold you back."

"But I don't want your money. I don't need you to take care of me. I certainly don't need you to save me."

"You're accusing me of a lot. The only thing that I'm guilty of is loving you."

Charisse sucked in her breath and pulled away. She almost grabbed her pocketbook and ran out of the restaurant. Being stuck in Tennessee was definitely not the answer.

"Tell me that you don't love me. I can see it in your eyes. I want to be honest with our feelings for each other."

Charisse closed her eyes and could feel the pounding of her heart. He couldn't know the truth. He mustn't. She would push away her secret. Eventually he would forget and move on.

"Charisse?" Brent said her name with enough pain in his voice to make her want to cry.

She remembered her mother's message. But she looked at the reality. Her mother had put off her dream for decades. Charisse couldn't accept that for herself.

She didn't respond. She clenched her hands under the table. Disappointment shone in his eyes, tearing at her heart. All she had to do was utter those three words.

She couldn't. She wouldn't.

Seven hours on the plane did nothing to ease the guilt and anxiety. Charisse pushed up the window shade by her seat and looked out on the busy tarmac at Heathrow Airport. When she got off this plane and disappeared into the heart of London, a new life awaited.

A life without Brent.

She took a deep breath. For once, she refused to

listen to her gut. Would she regret staying true to her philosophy?

"Ma'am, will you require assistance?" The flight attendant offered a slight smile as she waited.

Charisse shook her head. No, she was strong enough to go out there on her own. She scooted from between the seats, into the aisle with the other departing passengers.

The line through security was long, and one glance at the customs agents showed they were serious about their jobs. They fired their questions with no trace of a smile. Charisse looked down at the work visa and her passport. Hopefully she wouldn't have any problems getting through. It was nine in the morning, and she'd scheduled to meet her new client at noon.

Soon it was her turn to go through the process. She answered the questions about her purpose and where she was staying. The swanky hotel on the River Thames waterfront would be home for the week. Not bad after so much time spent worrying over where her next check would come from.

Charisse emerged from the restroom with her makeup repaired and a fresh blouse on. She'd kill for a cup of coffee, but it would have to wait. She scanned the signs with passenger names held by drivers.

She waved at the uniformed driver holding her last name.

"I hope that I didn't keep you waiting." She handed over her luggage.

The driver introduced himself. "No worries."

Once she made herself comfortable in the car, she retrieved her notes. Not that she needed to refresh her knowledge on her new client. She'd not only looked over the material that was sent but had done her own research.

Now she was ready to get to work, starting the new chapter that she'd convinced herself was necessary for her happiness.

Half an hour later, the driver pulled up to the hotel. Charisse stared out of the car window, looking up at the modern shiny building.

"I thought the meeting was at the office."

"There was a change of plan. Mr. Fielding will have the meeting here for your convenience."

The doorman opened her door, waiting for her to emerge.

Charisse was confused, but opted to act upon the invitation to enter the hotel's interior.

"Welcome to the Crisfield Hotel."

"Thank you," she murmured, completely in awe of the exquisite elegance of the hotel lobby. She followed the escort to the VIP check-in counter. She saw her sole suitcase waiting at the side of a bellman.

She was handed the room key card. "Your suite is on the tenth floor with the river view."

"I'm surprised that a room is ready." She took the key card, grateful to be able to get into her room before the meeting.

"Have an enjoyable stay, Ms. Sanford."

Charisse headed to the room with the bellman in tow. He insisted on carrying her luggage, and she felt silly but decided to go with the tradition.

After she'd tipped him and closed the door, she entered the suite and stopped. What she assumed was a junior suite with a king-size bed and a small sitting room turned out to be a full-size suite with a living room, dining area and kitchenette.

"So this is the difference of a client with deep pockets." She sank into the couch, putting her feet on the table in front of her.

She admired the room, running her gaze over the paintings and decorative pieces, including the vase of flowers.

"Flowers?" She stood and went to the large bouquet of red roses.

This was definitely not part of the hotel decor. She spied the small square note that was planted in the middle of the floral arrangement.

"Not giving up" was written in Brent's handwriting.

"Oh, Brent, you have no idea how much I miss you." She ran her finger over the note, wishing that it was his face instead.

She left the bouquet in place, although she wanted to push it out of sight. The flowers perfumed the air with a lazy, seductive scent. She didn't want any reminders to pull at her heart.

The phone in the room rang. She stretched for the handset.

"Good morning," she answered, with a slight questioning tone.

"Ms. Sanford, this is Patricia Clarke, Mr. Fielding's secretary. We will be meeting in his suite on the fifteenth floor in thirty minutes."

"What's the room number?"

"It's the entire floor. You'll have to go to the lobby and use the designated elevator."

Charisse bit back the "Wow."

After she hung up, she raced into the bedroom. The

linens looked crisp and inviting. No time to rest. She wanted to look alert and ready to go.

She'd changed her blouse, but now she felt compelled to wear an entirely new outfit. The very British nasal tone of the secretary motivated her to go traditional. She pulled off the pantsuit and instead grabbed a slim-fitting skirt and white shirt that subtly opened at the neck, where she fitted a single strand of pearls. The sleeves were three-quarter-length with big cuffs.

Instead of wearing her hair down, as she usually did, she pulled it into a ponytail. Gone was the casual American. She was now the international traveler and savvy businesswoman ready to take on her first British client.

Her putzing around ate up the thirty minutes. It was time to go. She followed the secretary's instructions to the specially reserved elevator.

She couldn't remember the last time she'd seen an elevator operator. For the ride up the fifteen floors, she pondered whether she had to tip him or not.

The doors opened, and a young woman stepped in and offered her a stiff handshake.

"I'm Charisse."

"I'm Patricia. This way, please."

Charisse only felt the soft breeze of the elevator doors closing. They'd stepped into a foyer that led directly into an apartment. There was no way that this large area with high ceilings and rooms at either end of the space could be called a suite. Even without a full tour, she was certain that her entire apartment could fit into the suite, with square footage to spare.

"Mr. Fielding, Charisse has arrived." The secretary

motioned toward a dining table that looked more like a board table.

Her client stood with a warm, welcoming smile.

"Good afternoon," she said, her voice cracking.

"Charisse, good to see you. You look well considering the long flight." He pulled out the chair closest to him. "I'll make the quick introductions. To my right is Dora Steinbaum, she runs the Fashion Forward Agency in New York and Los Angeles. At the head of the table is my second-in-command, Leticia Lumley. And on my left is my secretary."

"Hello, everyone." This time Charisse cleared her throat. She didn't want to come across as weak-sounding, even though she was a tad intimated by the power around the table.

For the next hour, she presented her plan for the chocolate company. Everything that she had learned in a formal setting, tips that she'd picked up from her years of experience and pearls of wisdom from Jake all came together. Her nerves were barely intact, but she drummed up the strength to finish on a high note.

By the time she left that afternoon to head back to her room, Charisse couldn't help but feel successful. Walking through the hotel lobby in a city where she knew no one, she began to panic. Did she have the stamina to continue working on this project for the next three months?

"Can I give you a penny for your thoughts?"

Charisse's head snapped up. That voice, smooth and rich, with a strong Bostonian accent, was familiar. Her brain tried to understand that she was actually seeing Brent standing in front of her. Her heart was screaming its love, and her body's reaction was heated and powerful.

"I'm here, Charisse, for you." Brent walked over to her.

Charisse pushed the button on the elevator. They rode up in silence. Her motions felt automatic. The adrenaline made her hands shake. They got to her suite.

"I'm not coming in, baby." Brent stood there looking down at her. His gray-blue eyes swallowed her with love.

"Why?"

"I want more. I'm here to convince you of that. I don't want to be tempted to simply sleep with you. Charisse, I would never hurt you. I love you and your strong independence."

Charisse almost cried that he wouldn't wrap those strong arms around her. She wanted it all. Fear churned her stomach.

Life had no guarantees.

Brent nodded. "I guess I was wrong, again." He turned to leave.

"Don't go," she whispered, her throat dry. "You are my world. It scares me, but it scares me even more not to have you in my life. From the first time that I met you, I knew that I was in trouble. Now I know that it wasn't a bad thing to run from but a beautiful feeling to embrace."

Brent remained half turned. He didn't look at her. She moved to stand directly in front of him. She tiptoed and kissed his mouth. She lingered, craving the touch of his lips.

"Brent Thatcher," she whispered, "I love you with all my heart."

Epilogue

Charisse sat on the floor of her office. The room, devoid of furniture and decorations, seemed larger but lacked any oomph. Yet it was the empty canvas that attracted her and helped spin the story of New Vision.

Many ideas had whirled into shape between these walls. Although she had a small staff, they had the enthusiasm and work ethic of a staff of one hundred. They'd all taken their baby steps in full view of each other, falling, tripping, but eventually teetering and balancing with swelling pride.

Brent entered the room and gently engulfed her in his arms. "Would you please come out and join the party?"

"I know, but look at me. I'm a blubbering mess." Charisse wiped away the tears that spewed as if from a leaky valve.

"It's not like Tracy and Jo aren't sobbing their hearts

out, either. They've even got Vicki grabbing a tissue or two."

"Maybe we need to change our names to Waterworks and Sobbing." Charisse turned to face Brent, cupping his face between her hands.

"There I'd have to protest as minority shareholder. New Vision says it all. We've merged for the better. I don't want to ever engulf and erase who you are and who you will become." His hands rested lightly on her hips.

"And I don't want you to ever be afraid that I won't be at your side for the journey. We're in this together, both here—" she touched his temple with her hand "—and here." She placed her hand over the right side of his chest.

"For that, I love you."

"I love you, too. And I love you even more now that you've reconciled with Harry." She kissed his mouth to show her gratitude. "I love you a smidgen more for your lovable mother and sweetheart of a father." She kissed his mouth again.

"Stop stirring the pot. I'm liable to go from a simmer to a full boil."

"We can't have that."

"No. Oh, and I don't know if you've thought about it, but my place is much closer to the office than yours."

"One move at a time. Your toothbrush already has its place in my bathroom."

This time Charisse pulled his head down to meet her eager mouth, now that she'd awakened her lips with his mouth. Their lips melted against each other in full harmony.

* * *

Brent covered Charisse's mouth, taking what she offered and sharing what he had to give. His heart soared with a new freedom. Every minute spent in her company, in her arms, thinking about her released him from all guilt about moving on and opened him to the possibilities of true happiness.

He escorted her back to their combined staff where friends and family celebrated their professional union. Now he was ready to make one more merger.

He waved his hand to quiet the room. From his pocket, he pulled out a small black box.

The group instantly quieted.

Charisse looked at his face and then down to the box. She cupped her mouth but not before he saw the wide grin.

"On your knee, son," his mom corrected.

Brent complied without hesitation. He wanted this to be right.

"Charisse, we have never been a couple who worked within the lines. But those were the qualities we admired in each other. You've awakened me to live in the moment, to forgive, to continue dreaming. All of those things wouldn't be the same without you by my side. Will you marry me?"

"Yes!" Charisse responded.

The room erupted with cheers. The popping sounds of champagne corks signaled that more celebrating was to be done.

* * * * *

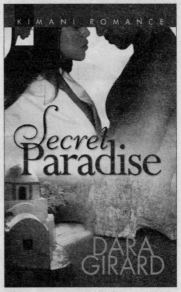

REQUEST YOUR FREE BOOKS!

2 FREE NOVELS
PLUS 2 FREE GIFTS!

KIMANI ROMANCE ™

Love's ultimate destination!